# LORELEI OF THE

# RED MIST

# LORELEI OF THE RED MIST

by Leigh Brackett and Ray Bradbury

*He died—and then awakened in a new body. He found himself on a world of bizarre loveliness, a powerful, rich man. He took pleasure in his turn of good luck ... until he discovered that his new body was hated by all on this strange planet, that his soul was owned by Rann, devil-goddess of Falga, who was using him for her own gain.*

The Company dicks were good. They were plenty good. Hugh Starke began to think maybe this time he wasn't going to get away with it.

His small stringy body hunched over the control bank, nursing the last ounce of power out of the Kallman. The hot night sky of Venus fled past the ports in tattered veils of indigo. Starke wasn't sure where he was any more. Venus was a frontier planet, and still mostly a big X, except to the Venusians—who weren't sending out any maps. He did know that he was getting dangerously close to the Mountains of White Cloud. The backbone of the planet, towering far into the stratosphere, magnetic trap, with God knew what beyond. Maybe even God wasn't sure.

But it looked like over the mountains or out. Death under the guns of the Terro-Venus Mines, Incorporated, Special Police, or back to the Luna cell blocks for life as an habitual felon.

Starke decided he would go over.

Whatever happened, he'd pulled off the biggest lone-wolf caper in history. The T-V Mines payroll ship, for close to a million credits. He cuddled the metal strongbox between his feet and grinned. It would be a long time before anybody equaled that.

His mass indicators began to jitter. Vaguely, a dim purple shadow in the sky ahead, the Mountains of White Cloud stood like a wall

5

against him. Starke checked the positions of the pursuing ships. There was no way through them. He said flatly, "All right, damn you," and sent the Kallman angling up into the thick blue sky.

He had no very clear memories after that. Crazy magnetic vagaries, always a hazard on Venus, made his instruments useless. He flew by the seat of his pants and he got over, and the T-V men didn't. He was free, with a million credits in his kick.

Far below in the virgin darkness he saw a sullen crimson smear on the night, as though someone had rubbed it with a bloody thumb. The Kallman dipped toward it. The control bank flickered with blue flame, the jet timers blew, and then there was just the screaming of air against the falling hull.

Hugh Starke sat still and waited....

He knew, before he opened his eyes, that he was dying. He didn't feel any pain, he didn't feel anything, but he knew just the same. Part of him was cut loose. He was still there, but not attached any more.

He raised his eyelids. There was a ceiling. It was a long way off. It was black stone veined with smoky reds and ambers. He had never seen it before.

His head was tilted toward the right. He let his gaze move down that way. There were dim tapestries, more of the black stone, and three tall archways giving onto a balcony. Beyond the balcony was a sky veiled and clouded with red mist. Under the mist, spreading away from a murky line of cliffs, was an ocean. It wasn't water and it didn't have any waves on it, but there was nothing else to call it. It burned, deep down inside itself, breathing up the red fog. Little angry bursts of flame coiled up under the flat surface, sending circles of sparks flaring out like ripples from a dropped stone.

He closed his eyes and frowned and moved his head restively. There was the texture of fur against his skin. Through the cracks of his eyelids he saw that he lay on a high bed piled with silks and soft tanned pelts. His body was covered. He was rather glad he couldn't see it. It didn't matter because he wouldn't be using it any more anyway, and it hadn't been such a hell of a body to begin with. But he was used to it, and he didn't want to see it now, the way he knew it would have to look.

He looked along over the foot of the bed, and he saw the woman.

She sat watching him from a massive carved chair softened with a single huge white pelt like a drift of snow. She smiled, and let him look. A pulse began to beat under his jaw, very feebly.

She was tall and sleek and insolently curved. She wore a sort of tabard of pale grey spider-silk, held to her body by a jeweled girdle, but it was just a nice piece of ornamentation. Her face was narrow, finely cut, secret, faintly amused. Her lips, her eyes, and her flowing silken hair were all the same pale cool shade of aquamarine.

Her skin was white, with no hint of rose. Her shoulders, her forearms, the long flat curve of her thighs, the pale-green tips of her breasts, were dusted with tiny particles that glistened like powdered diamond. She sparkled softly like a fairy thing against the snowy fur, a creature of foam and moonlight and clear shallow water. Her eyes never left his, and they were not human, but he knew that they would have done things to him if he had had any feeling below the neck.

\*

He started to speak. He had no strength to move his tongue. The woman leaned forward, and as though her movement were a signal four men rose from the tapestried shadows by the wall. They were like her. Their eyes were pale and strange like hers.

She said, in liquid High Venusian, "You're dying, in this body. But *you* will not die. You will sleep now, and wake in a strange body, in a strange place. Don't be afraid. My mind will be with yours, I'll guide you, don't be afraid. I can't explain now, there isn't time, but don't be afraid."

He drew back his thin lips baring his teeth in what might have been a smile. If it was, it was wolfish and bitter, like his face.

The woman's eyes began to pour coolness into his skull. They were like two little rivers running through the channels of his own eyes, spreading in silver-green quiet across the tortured surface of his brain. His brain relaxed. It lay floating on the water, and then the twin streams became one broad flowing stream, and his mind, or ego, the thing that was intimately himself, vanished along it.

It took him a long, long time to regain consciousness. He felt as though he'd been shaken until pieces of him were scattered all over inside. Also, he had an instinctive premonition that the minute he woke up he would be sorry he had. He took it easy, putting himself together.

He remembered his name, Hugh Starke. He remembered the mining asteroid where he was born. He remembered the Luna cell blocks where he had once come near dying. There wasn't much to choose between them. He remembered his face decorating half the bulletin boards between Mercury and The Belt. He remembered hearing about himself over the telecasts, stuff to frighten babies with, and he thought of himself committing his first crime—a stunted scrawny kid of eighteen swinging a spanner on a grown man who was trying to steal his food.

The rest of it came fast, then. The T-V Mines job, the getaway that didn't get, the Mountains of White Cloud. The crash....

The woman.

That did it. His brain leaped shatteringly. Light, feeling, a naked sense of reality swept over him. He lay perfectly still with his eyes shut, and his mind clawed at the picture of the shining woman with sea-green hair and the sound of her voice saying, *You will not die, you will wake in a strange body, don't be afraid....*

He was afraid. His skin pricked and ran cold with it. His stomach knotted with it. His skin, his stomach, and yet somehow they didn't feel just right, like a new coat that hasn't shaped to you....

He opened his eyes, a cautious crack.

He saw a body sprawled on its side in dirty straw. The body belonged to him, because he could feel the straw pricking it, and the itch of little things that crawled and ate and crawled again.

It was a powerful body, rangy and flat-muscled, much bigger than his old one. It had obviously not been starved the first twenty-some years of its life. It was stark naked. Weather and violence had written history on it, wealed white marks on leathery bronze, but nothing seemed to be missing. There was black hair on its chest and thighs and forearms, and its hands were lean and sinewy for killing.

It was a human body. That was something. There were so many other things it might have been that his racial snobbery wouldn't call human. Like the nameless shimmering creature who smiled with strange pale lips.

Starke shut his eyes again.

He lay, the intangible self that was Hugh Starke, bellied down in the darkness of the alien shell, quiet, indrawn, waiting. Panic crept up on its soft black paws. It walked around the crouching ego and sniffed and patted and nuzzled, whining, and then struck with its raking claws. After a while it went away, empty.

The lips that were now Starke's lips twitched in a thin, cruel smile. He had done six months once in the Luna solitary crypts. If a man could do that, and come out sane and on his two feet, he could stand anything. Even this.

9

# LORELEI OF THE RED MIST

It came to him then, rather deflatingly, that the woman and her four companions had probably softened the shock by hypnotic suggestion. His subconscious understood and accepted the change. It was only his conscious mind that was superficially scared to death.

Hugh Starke cursed the woman with great thoroughness, in seven languages and some odd dialects. He became healthily enraged that any dame should play around with him like that. Then he thought, What the hell, I'm alive. And it looks like I got the best of the trade-in!

He opened his eyes again, secretly, on his new world.

*

He lay at one end of a square stone hall, good sized, with two straight lines of pillars cut from some dark Venusian wood. There were long crude benches and tables. Fires had been burning on round brick hearths spaced between the pillars. They were embers now. The smoke climbed up, tarnishing the gold and bronze of shields hung on the walls and pediments, dulling the blades of longswords, the spears, the tapestries and hides and trophies.

It was very quiet in the hall. Somewhere outside of it there was fighting going on. Heavy, vicious fighting. The noise of it didn't touch the silence, except to make it deeper.

There were two men besides Starke in the hall.

They were close to him, on a low dais. One of them sat in a carved high seat, not moving, his big scarred hands flat on the table in front of him. The other crouched on the floor by his feet. His head was bent forward so that his mop of lint-white hair hid his face and the harp between his thighs. He was a little man, a swamp-edger from his albino coloring. Starke looked back at the man in the chair.

The man spoke harshly. "Why doesn't she send word?"

The harp gave out a sudden bitter chord. That was all.

Starke hardly noticed. His whole attention was drawn to the speaker. His heart began to pound. His muscles coiled and lay ready. There was a bitter taste in his mouth. He recognized it. It was hate.

He had never seen the man before, but his hands twitched with the urge to kill.

He was big, nearly seven feet, and muscled like a draft horse. But his body, naked above a gold-bossed leather kilt, was lithe and quick as a greyhound in spite of its weight. His face was square, strong-boned, weathered, and still young. It was a face that had laughed a lot once, and liked wine and pretty girls. It had forgotten those things now, except maybe the wine. It was drawn and cruel with pain, a look as of something in a cage. Starke had seen that look before, in the Luna blocks. There was a thick white scar across the man's forehead. Under it his blue eyes were sunken and dark behind half-closed lids. The man was blind.

Outside, in the distance, men screamed and died.

Starke had been increasingly aware of a soreness and stricture around his neck. He raised a hand, careful not to rustle the straw. His fingers found a long tangled beard, felt under it, and touched a band of metal.

Starke's new body wore a collar, like a vicious dog.

There was a chain attached to the collar. Starke couldn't find any fastening. The business had been welded on for keeps. His body didn't seem to have liked it much. The neck was galled and chafed.

The blood began to crawl up hot into Starke's head. He'd worn chains before. He didn't like them. Especially around the neck.

A door opened suddenly at the far end of the hall. Fog and red daylight spilled in across the black stone floor. A man came in. He was big, half naked, blond, and bloody. His long blade trailed harshly

11

on the flags. His chest was laid open to the bone and he held the wound together with his free hand.

"Word from Beudag," he said. "They've driven us back into the city, but so far we're holding the Gate."

No one spoke. The little man nodded his white head. The man with the slashed chest turned and went out again, closing the door.

A peculiar change came over Starke at the mention of the name Beudag. He had never heard it before, but it hung in his mind like a spear point, barbed with strange emotion. He couldn't identify the feeling, but it brushed the blind man aside. The hot simple hatred cooled. Starke relaxed in a sort of icy quiet, deceptively calm as a sleeping cobra. He didn't question this. He waited, for Beudag.

The blind man struck his hands down suddenly on the table and stood up. "Romna," he said, "give me my sword."

The little man looked at him. He had milk-blue eyes and a face like a friendly bulldog. He said, "Don't be a fool, Faolan."

Faolan said softly, "Damn you. Give me my sword."

Men were dying outside the hall, and not dying silently. Faolan's skin was greasy with sweat. He made a sudden, darting grab toward Romna.

Romna dodged him. There were tears in his pale eyes. He said brutally, "You'd only be in the way. Sit down."

"I can find the point," Faolan said, "to fall on it."

Romna's voice went up to a harsh scream. "Shut up. Shut up and sit down."

Faolan caught the edge of the table and bent over it. He shivered and closed his eyes, and the tears ran out hot under the lids. The bard turned away, and his harp cried out like a woman.

Faolan drew a long sighing breath. He straightened slowly, came round the carved high seat, and walked steadily toward Starke.

"You're very quiet, Conan," he said. "What's the matter? You ought to be happy, Conan. You ought to laugh and rattle your chain. You're going to get what you wanted. Are you sad because you haven't a mind any more, to understand that with?"

He stopped and felt with one sandaled foot across the straw until he touched Starke's thigh. Starke lay motionless.

"Conan," said the blind man gently, pressing Starke's belly with his foot. "Conan the dog, the betrayer, the butcher, the knife in the back. Remember what you did at Falga, Conan? No, you don't remember now. I've been a little rough with you, and you don't remember any more. But I remember, Conan. As long as I live in darkness, I'll remember."

*

Romna stroked the harp strings and they wept, savage tears for strong men dead of treachery. Low music, distant but not soft. Faolan began to tremble, a shallow animal twitching of the muscles. The flesh of his face was drawn, iron shaping under the hammer. Quite suddenly he went down on his knees. His hands struck Starke's shoulders, slid inward to the throat, and locked there.

Outside, the sound of fighting had died away.

Starke moved, very quickly. As though he had seen it and knew it was there, his hand swept out and gathered in the slack of the heavy chain and swung it.

It started out to be a killing blow. Starke wanted with all his heart to beat Faolan's brains out. But at the last second he pulled it, slapping the big man with exquisite judgment across the back of the head. Faolan grunted and fell sideways, and by that time Romna had come up. He had dropped his harp and drawn a knife. His eyes were startled.

# LORELEI OF THE RED MIST

Starke sprang up. He backed off, swinging the slack of the chain warningly. His new body moved magnificently. Outside everything was fine, but inside his psycho-neural setup had exploded into civil war. He was furious with himself for not having killed Faolan. He was furious with himself for losing control enough to want to kill a man without reason. He hated Faolan. He did not hate Faolan because he didn't know him well enough. Starke's trained, calculating, unemotional brain was at grips with a tidal wave of baseless emotion.

He hadn't realized it was baseless until his mental monitor, conditioned through years of bitter control, had stopped him from killing. Now he remembered the woman's voice saying, *My mind will be with yours, I'll guide you....*

Catspaw, huh? Just a hired hand, paid off with a new body in return for two lives. Yeah, two. This Beudag, whoever he was. Starke knew now what that cold alien emotion had been leading up to.

"Hold it," said Starke hoarsely. "Hold everything. *Catspaw! You green-eyed she-devil! You picked the wrong guy this time.*"

Just for a fleeting instant he saw her again, leaning forward with her hair like running water across the soft foam-sparkle of her shoulders. Her sea-pale eyes were full of mocking laughter, and a direct, provocative admiration. Starke heard her quite plainly:

"You may not have any choice, Hugh Starke. They know Conan, even if you don't. Besides, it's of no great importance. The end will be the same for them—it's just a matter of time. You can save your new body or not, as you wish." She smiled. "I'd like it if you did. It's a good body. I knew it, before Conan's mind broke and left it empty."

A sudden thought came to Starke. "My box, the million credits."

14

"Come and get them." She was gone. Starke's mind was clear, with no alien will tramping around in it. Faolan crouched on the floor, holding his head. He said:

"Who spoke?"

Romna the bard stood staring. His lips moved, but no sound came out.

Starke said, "I spoke. Me, Hugh Starke. I'm not Conan, and I never heard of Falga, and I'll brain the first guy that comes near me."

Faolan stayed motionless, his face blank, his breath sobbing in his throat. Romna began to curse, very softly, not as though he were thinking about it. Starke watched them.

Down the hall the doors burst open. The heavy reddish mist coiled in with the daylight across the flags, and with them a press of bodies hot from battle, bringing a smell of blood.

Starke felt the heart contract in the hairy breast of the body named Conan, watching the single figure that led the pack.

Romna called out, "Beudag!"

She was tall. She was built and muscled like a lioness, and she walked with a flat-hipped arrogance, and her hair was like coiled flame. Her eyes were blue, hot and bright, as Faolan's might have been once. She looked like Faolan. She was dressed like him, in a leather kilt and sandals, her magnificent body bare above the waist. She carried a longsword slung across her back, the hilt standing above the left shoulder. She had been using it. Her skin was smeared with blood and grime. There was a long cut on her thigh and another across her flat belly, and bitter weariness lay on her like a burden in spite of her denial of it.

"We've stopped them, Faolan," she said. "They can't breach the Gate, and we can hold Crom Dhu as long as we have food. And the

15

sea feeds us." She laughed, but there was a hollow sound to it. "Gods, I'm tired!"

She halted then, below the dais. Her flame-blue gaze swept across Faolan, across Romna, and rose to meet Hugh Starke's, and stayed there.

The pulse began to beat under Starke's jaw again, and this time his body was strong, and the pulse was like a drum throbbing.

Romna said, "His mind has come back."

*

There was a long, hard silence. No one in the hall moved. Then the men back of Beudag, big brawny kilted warriors, began to close in on the dais, talking in low snarling undertones that rose toward a mob howl. Faolan rose up and faced them, and bellowed them to quiet.

"He's mine to take! Let him alone."

Beudag sprang up onto the dais, one beautiful flowing movement. "It isn't possible," she said. "His mind broke under torture. He's been a drooling idiot with barely the sense to feed himself. And now, suddenly, you say he's normal again?"

Starke said, "You know I'm normal. You can see it in my eyes."

"Yes."

He didn't like the way she said that. "Listen, my name is Hugh Starke. I'm an Earthman. This isn't Conan's brain come back. This is a new deal. I got shoved into this body. What it did before I got it I don't know, and I'm not responsible."

Faolan said, "He doesn't remember Falga. He doesn't remember the longships at the bottom of the sea." Faolan laughed.

Romna said quietly, "He didn't kill you, though. He could have, easily. Would Conan have spared you?"

16

Beudag said, "Yes, if he had a better plan. Conan's mind was like a snake. It crawled in the dark, and you never knew where it was going to strike."

Starke began to tell them how it happened, the chain swinging idly in his hand. While he was talking he saw a face reflected in a polished shield hung on a pillar. Mostly it was just a tangled black mass of hair, mounted on a frame of long, harsh, jutting bone. The mouth was sensuous, with a dark sort of laughter on it. The eyes were yellow. The cruel, brilliant yellow of a killer hawk.

Starke realized with a shock that the face belonged to him.

"A woman with pale green hair," said Beudag softly. "Rann," said Faolan, and Romna's harp made a sound like a high-priest's curse.

"Her people have that power," Romna said. "They can think a man's soul into a spider, and step on it."

"They have many powers. Maybe Rann followed Conan's mind, wherever it went, and told it what to say, and brought it back again."

"Listen," said Starke angrily. "I didn't ask...."

Suddenly, without warning, Romna drew Beudag's sword and threw it at Starke.

Starke dodged it. He looked at Romna with ugly yellow eyes. "That's fine. Chain me up so I can't fight and kill me from a distance." He did not pick up the sword. He'd never used one. The chain felt better, not being too different from a heavy belt or a length of cable, or the other chains he'd swung on occasion.

Romna said, "Is that Conan?"

Faolan snarled, "What happened?"

"Romna threw my sword at Conan. He dodged it, and left it on the ground." Beudag's eyes were narrowed. "Conan could catch a flying sword by the hilt, and he was the best fighter on the Red Sea, barring you, Faolan."

"He's trying to trick us. Rann guides him."

"The hell with Rann!" Starke clashed his chain. "She wants me to kill the both of you, I still don't know why. All right. I could have killed Faolan, easy. But I'm not a killer. I never put down anyone except to save my own neck. So I didn't kill him in spite of Rann. And I don't want any part of you, or Rann either. All I want is to get the hell out of here!"

Beudag said, "His accent isn't Conan's. And the look in his eyes is different, too." Her voice had an odd note in it. Romna glanced at her. He fingered a few rippling chords on his harp, and said:

"There's one way you could tell for sure."

A sullen flush began to burn on Beudag's cheekbones. Romna slid unobtrusively out of reach. His eyes danced with malicious laughter.

Beudag smiled, the smile of an angry cat, all teeth and no humor. Suddenly she walked toward Starke, her head erect, her hands swinging loose and empty at her sides. Starke tensed warily, but the blood leaped pleasantly in his borrowed veins.

Beudag kissed him.

Starke dropped the chain. He had something better to do with his hands.

After a while he raised his head for breath, and she stepped back, and whispered wonderingly,

"It isn't Conan."

*

The hall had been cleared. Starke had washed and shaved himself. His new face wasn't bad. Not bad at all. In fact, it was pretty damn good. And it wasn't known around the System. It was a face that could own a million credits and no questions asked. It was a face that could have a lot of fun on a million credits.

All he had to figure out now was a way to save the neck the face was mounted on, and get his million credits back from that beautiful she-devil named Rann.

He was still chained, but the straw had been cleaned up and he wore a leather kilt and a pair of sandals. Faolan sat in his high seat nursing a flagon of wine. Beudag sprawled wearily on a fur rug beside him. Romna sat cross-legged, his eyes veiled sleepily, stroking soft wandering music out of his harp. He looked fey. Starke knew his swamp-edgers. He wasn't surprised.

"This man is telling the truth," Romna said. "But there's another mind touching his. Rann's, I think. Don't trust him."

Faolan growled, "I couldn't trust a god in Conan's body."

Starke said, "What's the setup? All the fighting out there, and this Rann dame trying to plant a killer on the inside. And what happened at Falga? I never heard of this whole damn ocean, let alone a place called Falga."

The bard swept his hand across the strings. "I'll tell you, Hugh Starke. And maybe you won't want to stay in that body any longer."

Starke grinned. He glanced at Beudag. She was watching him with a queer intensity from under lowered lids. Starke's grin changed. He began to sweat. Get rid of this body, hell! It was really a body. His own stringy little carcass had never felt like this.

The bard said, "In the beginning, in the Red Sea, was a race of people having still their fins and scales. They were amphibious, but after a while part of this race wanted to remain entirely on land. There was a quarrel, and a battle, and some of the people left the sea forever. They settled along the shore. They lost their fins and most of their scales. They had great mental powers and they loved ruling. They subjugated the human peoples and kept them almost in slavery.

19

They hated their brothers who still lived in the sea, and their brothers hated them.

"After a time a third people came to the Red Sea. They were rovers from the North. They raided and rieved and wore no man's collar. They made a settlement on Crom Dhu, the Black Rock, and built longships, and took toll of the coastal towns.

"But the slave people didn't want to fight against the rovers. They wanted to fight with them and destroy the sea-folk. The rovers were human, and blood calls to blood. And the rovers like to rule, too, and this is a rich country. Also, the time had come in their tribal development when they were ready to change from nomadic warriors to builders in their own country.

"So the rovers, and the sea-folk, and the slave-people who are caught between the two of them, began their struggle for the land."

The bard's fingers thrummed against the strings so that they beat like angry hearts. Starke saw that Beudag was still watching him, weighing every change of expression on his face. Romna went on:

"There was a woman named Rann, who had green hair and great beauty, and ruled the sea-folk. There was a man called Faolan of the Ships, and his sister Beudag, which means Dagger-in-the-Sheath, and they two ruled the outland rovers. And there was the man called Conan."

The harp crashed out like a sword-blade striking.

"Conan was a great fighter and a great lover. He was next under Faolan of the Ships, and Beudag loved him, and they were plighted. Then Conan was taken prisoner by the sea-folk during a skirmish, and Rann saw him—and Conan saw Rann."

Hugh Starke had a fleeting memory of Rann's face smiling, and her low voice saying, *It's a good body. I knew it, before....*

Beudag's eyes were two stones of blue vitriol under her narrow lids.

"Conan stayed a long time at Falga with Rann of the Red Sea. Then he came back to Crom Dhu, and said that he had escaped, and had discovered a way to take the longships into the harbor of Falga, at the back of Rann's fleet, and from there it would be easy to take the city, and Rann with it. And Conan and Beudag were married."

Starke's yellow hawk eyes slid over Beudag, sprawled like a young lioness in power and beauty. A muscle began to twitch under his cheekbone. Beudag flushed, a slow deep color. Her gaze did not waver.

"So the longships went out from Crom Dhu, across the Red Sea. And Conan led them into a trap at Falga, and more than half of them were sunk. Conan thought his ship was free, that he had Rann and all she'd promised him, but Faolan saw what had happened and went after him. They fought, and Conan laid his sword across Faolan's brow and blinded him; but Conan lost the fight. Beudag brought them home.

"Conan was chained naked in the market place. The people were careful not to kill him. From time to time other things were done to him. After a while his mind broke, and Faolan had him chained here in the hall, where he could hear him babble and play with his chain. It made the darkness easier to bear.

"But since Falga, things have gone badly from Crom Dhu. Too many men were lost, too many ships. Now Rann's people have us bottled up here. They can't break in, we can't break out. And so we stay, until...." The harp cried out a bitter question, and was still.

*

After a minute or two Starke said slowly, "Yeah, I get it. Stalemate for both of you. And Rann figured if I could kill off the leaders, your people might give up." He began to curse. "What a lousy, dirty, sneaking trick! And who told her she could use me...." He paused.

After all, he'd be dead now. After all, a new body, and a cool million credits. Ah, the hell with Rann. He hadn't asked her to do it. And he was nobody's hired killer. Where did she get off, sneaking around his mind, trying to make him do things he didn't even know about? Especially to someone like Beudag.

Still, Rann herself was nobody's crud.

And just where was Hugh Starke supposed to cut in on this deal? Cut was right. Probably with a longsword, right through the belly. Swell spot he was in, and a good three strikes on him already.

He was beginning to wish he'd never seen the T-V Mines payroll ship, because then he might never have seen the Mountains of White Cloud.

He said, because everybody seemed to be waiting for him to say something, "Usually when there's a deadlock like this, somebody calls in a third party. Isn't there somebody you can yell for?"

Faolan shook his rough red head. "The slave people might rise, but they haven't arms and they're not used to fighting. They'd only get massacred, and it wouldn't help us any."

"What about those other—uh—people that live in the sea? And just what is that sea, anyhow? Some radiation from it wrecked my ship and got me into this bloody mess."

Beudag said lazily, "I don't know what it is. The seas our forefathers sailed on were water, but this is different. It will float a ship, if you know how to build the hull—very thin, of a white metal we mine from the foothills. But when you swim in it, it's like being in a cloud of bubbles. It tingles, and the farther down you go in it the stranger it gets, dark and full of fire. I stay down for hours sometimes, hunting the beasts that live there."

Starke said, "For hours? You have diving suits, then."

"What are they?" Starke told her. She shook her head, laughing. "Why weigh yourself down that way? There's no trouble to breathe in this ocean."

"For cripesake," said Starke. "Well I'll be damned. Must be a heavy gas, then, radioactive, surface tension under atmospheric pressure, enough to float a light hull, and high oxygen content without any dangerous mixture. Well, well. Okay, why doesn't somebody go down and see if the sea-people will help? They don't like Rann's branch of the family, you said."

"They don't like us, either," said Faolan. "We stay out of the southern part of the sea. They wreck our ships, sometimes." His bitter mouth twisted in a smile. "Did you want to go to them for help?"

Starke didn't quite like the way Faolan sounded. "It was just a suggestion," he said.

Beudag rose, stretching, wincing as the stiffened wounds pulled her flesh. "Come, on, Faolan. Let's sleep."

He rose and laid his hand on her shoulder. Romna's harpstrings breathed a subtle little mockery of sound. The bard's eyes were veiled and sleepy. Beudag did not look at Starke, called Conan.

Starke said, "What about me?"

"You stay chained," said Faolan. "There's plenty of time to think. As long as we have food—and the sea feeds us."

He followed Beudag, through a curtained entrance to the left. Romna got up, slowly, slinging the harp over one white shoulder. He stood looking steadily into Starke's eyes in the dying light of the fires.

"I don't know," he murmured.

Starke waited, not speaking. His face was without expression.

"Conan we knew. Starke we don't know. Perhaps it would have been better if Conan had come back." He ran his thumb absently over the hilt of the knife in his girdle. "I don't know. Perhaps it would have been better for all of us if I'd cut your throat before Beudag came in."

Starke's mouth twitched. It was not exactly a smile.

"You see," said the bard seriously, "to you, from Outside, none of this is important, except as it touches you. But we live in this little world. We die in it. To us, it's important."

The knife was in his hand now. It leaped up glittering into the dregs of the firelight, and fell, and leaped again.

"You fight for yourself, Hugh Starke. Rann also fights through you. I don't know."

Starke's gaze did not waver.

Romna shrugged and put away the knife. "It is written of the gods," he said, sighing. "I hope they haven't done a bad job of the writing."

He went out. Starke began to shiver slightly. It was completely quiet in the hall. He examined his collar, the rivets, every separate link of the chain, the staple to which it was fixed. Then he sat down on the fur rug provided for him in place of the straw. He put his face in his hands and cursed, steadily, for several minutes, and then struck his fists down hard on the floor. After that he lay down and was quiet. He thought Rann would speak to him. She did not.

The silent black hours that walked across his heart were worse than any he had spent in the Luna crypts.

*

She came soft-shod, bearing a candle. Beudag, the Dagger-in-the-Sheath. Starke was not sleeping. He rose and stood waiting. She set the candle on the table and came, not quite to him, and stopped. She wore a length of thin white cloth twisted loosely at the waist and dropping to her ankles. Her body rose out of it straight and lovely, touched mystically with shadows in the little wavering light.

"Who are you?" she whispered. "What are you?"

"A man. Not Conan. Maybe not Hugh Starke any more. Just a man."

"I loved the man called Conan, until...." She caught her breath, and moved closer. She put her hand on Starke's arm. The touch went through him like white fire. The warm clean healthy fragrance of her tasted sweet in his throat. Her eyes searched his.

"If Rann has such great powers, couldn't it be that Conan was forced to do what he did? Couldn't it be that Rann took his mind and moulded it her way, perhaps without his knowing it?"

"It could be."

"Conan was hot-tempered and quarrelsome, but he...."

Starke said slowly, "I don't think you could have loved him if he hadn't been straight."

Her hand lay still on his forearm. She stood looking at him, and then her hand began to tremble, and in a moment she was crying, making no noise about it. Starke drew her gently to him. His eyes blazed yellowly in the candlelight.

"Woman's tears," she said impatiently, after a bit. She tried to draw away. "I've been fighting too long, and losing, and I'm tired."

He let her step back, not far. "Do all the women of Crom Dhu fight like men?"

"If they want to. There have always been shield-maidens. And since Falga, I would have had to fight anyway, to keep from thinking." She touched the collar on Starke's neck. "And from seeing."

He thought of Conan in the market square, and Conan shaking his chain and gibbering in Faolan's hall, and Beudag watching it. Starke's fingers tightened. He slid his palms upward along the smooth muscles of her arms, across the straight, broad planes of her shoulders, onto her neck, the proud strength of it pulsing under his hands. Her hair fell loose. He could feel the redness of it burning him.

She whispered, "You don't love me."

"No."

"You're an honest man, Hugh Starke."

"You want me to kiss you."

"Yes."

"You're an honest woman, Beudag."

Her lips were hungry, passionate, touched with the bitterness of tears. After a while Starke blew out the candle....

"I could love you, Beudag."

"Not the way I mean."

"The way you mean. I've never said that to any woman before. But you're not like any woman before. And—I'm a different man."

"Strange—so strange. Conan, and yet not Conan."

"I could love you, Beudag—if I lived."

Harpstrings gave a thrumming sigh in the darkness, the faintest whisper of sound. Beudag started, sighed, and rose from the fur rug. In a minute she had found flint and steel and got the candle lighted. Romna the bard stood in the curtained doorway, watching them.

Presently he said, "You're going to let him go."

Beudag said, "Yes."

Romna nodded. He did not seem surprised. He walked across the dais, laying his harp on the table, and went into another room. He came back almost at once with a hacksaw.

"Bend your neck," he said to Starke.

The metal of the collar was soft. When it was cut through Starke got his fingers under it and bent the ends outward, without trouble. His old body could never have done that. His old body could never

26

have done a lot of things. He figured Rann hadn't cheated him. Not much.

He got up, looking at Beudag. Beudag's head was dropped forward, her face veiled behind shining hair.

"There's only one possible way out of Crom Dhu," she said. There was no emotion in her voice. "There's a passage leading down through the rock to a secret harbor, just large enough to moor a skiff or two. Perhaps, with the night and the fog, you can slip through Rann's blockade. Or you can go aboard one of her ships, for Falga." She picked up the candle. "I'll take you down."

"Wait," Starke said. "What about you?"

She glanced at him, surprised. "I'll stay, of course."

He looked into her eyes. "It's going to be hard to know each other that way."

"You can't stay here, Hugh Starke. The people would tear you to pieces the moment you went into the street. They may even storm the hall, to take you. Look here." She set the candle down and led him to a narrow window, drawing back the hide that covered it.

Starke saw narrow twisting streets dropping steeply toward the sullen sea. The longships were broken and sunk in the harbor. Out beyond, riding lights flickering in the red fog, were other ships. Rann's ships.

"Over there," said Beudag, "is the mainland. Crom Dhu is connected to it by a tongue of rock. The sea-folk hold the land beyond it, but we can hold the rock bridge as long as we live. We have enough water, enough food from the sea. But there's no soil nor game on Crom Dhu. We'll be naked after a while, without leather or flax, and we'll have scurvy without grain and fruit. We're beaten, unless the gods send us a miracle. And we're beaten because of what was done at Falga. You can see how the people feel."

27

Starke looked at the dark streets and the silent houses leaning on each other's shoulders, and the mocking lights out in the fog. "Yeah," he said. "I can see."

"Besides, there's Faolan. I don't know whether he believes your story. I don't know whether it would matter."

Starke nodded. "But you won't come with me?"

She turned away sharply and picked up the candle again. "Are you coming, Romna?"

The bard nodded. He slung his harp over his shoulder. Beudag held back the curtain of a small doorway far to the side. Starke went through it and Romna followed, and Beudag went ahead with the candle. No one spoke.

*

They went along a narrow passage, past store rooms and armories. They paused once while Starke chose a knife, and Romna whispered: "Wait!" He listened intently. Starke and Beudag strained their ears along with him. There was no sound in the sleeping dun. Romna shrugged. "I thought I heard sandals scraping stone," he said. They went on.

The passage lay behind a wooden door. It led downward steeply through the rock, a single narrow way without side galleries or branches. In some places there were winding steps. It ended, finally, in a flat ledge low to the surface of the cove, which was a small cavern closed in with the black rock. Beudag set the candle down.

There were two little skiffs built of some light metal moored to rings in the ledge. Two long sweeps leaned against the cave wall. They were of a different metal, oddly vaned. Beudag laid one across the thwarts of the nearest boat. Then she turned to Starke. Romna hung back in the shadows by the tunnel mouth.

Beudag said quietly, "Goodbye, man without a name."

28

"It has to be goodbye."

"I'm leader now, in Faolan's place. Besides, these are my people." Her fingers tightened on his wrists. "If you could...." Her eyes held a brief blaze of hope. Then she dropped her head and said, "I keep forgetting you're not one of us. Goodbye."

"Goodbye, Beudag."

Starke put his arms around her. He found her mouth, almost cruelly. Her arms were tight about him, her eyes half closed and dreaming. Starke's hands slip upward, toward her throat, and locked on it.

She bent back, her body like a steel bow. Her eyes got fire in them, looking into Starke's but only for a moment. His fingers pressed expertly on the nerve centers. Beudag's head fell forward limply, and then Romna was on Starke's back and his knife was pricking Starke's throat.

Starke caught his wrist and turned the blade away. Blood ran onto his chest, but the cut was not into the artery. He threw himself backward onto the stone. Romna couldn't get clear in time. The breath went out of him in a rushing gasp. He didn't let go of the knife. Starke rolled over. The little man didn't have a chance with him. He was tough and quick, but Starke's sheer size smothered him. Starke could remember when Romna would not have seemed small to him. He hit the bard's jaw with his fist. Romna's head cracked hard against the stone. He let go of the knife. He seemed to be through fighting. Starke got up. He was sweating, breathing heavily, not because of his exertion. His mouth was glistening and eager, like a dog's. His muscles twitched, his belly was hot and knotted with excitement. His yellow eyes had a strange look.

He went back to Beudag.

# LORELEI OF THE RED MIST

She lay on the black rock, on her back. Candlelight ran pale gold across her brown skin, skirting the sharp strong hollows between her breasts and under the arching rim of her rib-case. Starke knelt, across her body, his weight pressed down against her harsh breathing. He stared at her. Sweat stood out on his face. He took her throat between his hands again.

He watched the blood grow dark in her checks. He watched the veins coil on her forehead. He watched the redness blacken in her lips. She fought a little, very vaguely, like someone moving in a dream. Starke breathed hoarsely, animal-like, through an open mouth.

Then, gradually his body became rigid. His hands froze, not releasing pressure, but not adding any. His yellow eyes widened. It was as though he were trying to see Beudag's face and it was hidden in dense clouds.

Back of him, back in the tunnel, was the soft, faint whisper of sandals on uneven rock. Sandals, walking slowly. Starke did not hear. Beudag's face glimmered deep in a heavy mist below him, a blasphemy of a face, distorted, blackened.

Starke's hands began to open.

They opened slowly. Muscles stood like coiled ropes in his arms and shoulders, as though he moved them against heavy weights. His lips peeled back from his teeth. He bent his neck, and sweat dropped from his face and glittered on Beudag's breast.

Starke was now barely touching Beudag's neck. She began to breathe again, painfully.

Starke began to laugh. It was not nice laughter. "Rann," he whispered. "Rann, you she-devil." He half fell away from Beudag and stood up, holding himself against the wall. He was shaking violently. "I wouldn't use your hate for killing, so you tried to use my passion."

He cursed her in a flat sibilant whisper. He had never in his profane life really cursed anyone before.

He heard an echo of laughter dancing in his brain.

Starke turned. Faolan of the Ships stood in the tunnel mouth. His head was bent, listening, his blind dark eyes fixed on Starke as though he saw him.

*

Faolan said softly "I hear you, Starke. I hear the other breathing, but they don't speak."

"They're all right. I didn't mean to do...."

Faolan smiled. He stepped out on the narrow ledge. He knew where he was going, and his smile was not pleasant.

"I heard your steps in the passage beyond my room. I knew Beudag was leading you, and where, and why. I would have been here sooner, but it's a slow way in the dark."

The candle lay in his path. He felt the heat of it close to his leg, and stopped and felt for it, and ground it out. It was dark, then. Very dark, except for a faint smudgy glow from the scrap of ocean that lay along the cave floor.

"It doesn't matter," Faolan said, "as long as I came in time."

Starke shifted his weight warily. "Faolan...."

"I wanted you alone. On this night of all nights I wanted you alone. Beudag fights in my place now, Conan. My manhood needs proving."

Starke strained his eyes in the gloom, measuring the ledge, measuring the place where the skiff was moored. He didn't want to fight Faolan. In Faolan's place he would have felt the same. Starke understood perfectly. He didn't hate Faolan, he didn't want to kill him, and he was afraid of Rann's power over him when his emotions got control. You couldn't keep a determined man from killing you and still be uninvolved emotionally. Starke would be damned if he'd kill anyone to suit Rann.

He moved, silently, trying to slip past Faolan on the outside and get into the skiff. Faolan gave no sign of hearing him. Starke did not breathe. His sandals came down lighter than snowflakes. Faolan did not swerve. He would pass Starke with a foot to spare. They came abreast.

Faolan's hand shot out and caught in Starke's long black hair. The blind man laughed softly and closed in.

Starke swung one from the floor. Do it the quickest way and get clear. But Faolan was fast. He came in so swiftly that Starke's fist jarred harmlessly along his ribs. He was bigger than Starke, and heavier, and the darkness didn't bother him.

Starke bared his teeth. Do it quick, brother, and clear out! Or that green-eyed she-cat.... Faolan's brute bulk weighed him down. Faolan's arm crushed his neck. Faolan's fist was knocking his guts loose. Starke got moving.

He'd fought in a lot of places. He'd learned from stokers and tramps, Martian Low-Canalers, red-eyed Nahali in the running gutters of Lhi. He didn't use his knife. He used his knees and feet and elbows and his hands, fist and flat. It was a good fight. Faolan was a good fighter, but Starke knew more tricks.

One more, Starke thought. One more and he's out. He drew back for it, and his heel struck Romna, lying on the rock. He staggered, and Faolan caught him with a clean swinging blow. Starke fell backward against the cave wall. His head cracked the rock. Light flooded crimson across his brain and then paled and grew cooler, a wash of clear silver-green like water. He sank under it....

# LEIGH BRACKETT AND RAY BRADBURY

He was tired, desperately tired. His head ached. He wanted to rest, but he could feel that he was sitting up, doing something that had to be done. He opened his eyes.

He sat in the stern of a skiff. The long sweep was laid into its crutch, held like a tiller bar against his body. The blade of the sweep trailed astern in the red sea, and where the metal touched there was a spurt of silver fire and a swirling of brilliant motes. The skiff moved rapidly through the sullen fog, through a mist of blood in the hot Venusian night.

Beudag crouched in the bow, facing Starke. She was bound securely with strips of the white cloth she had worn. Bruises showed dark on her throat. She was watching Starke with the intent, unwinking, perfectly expressionless gaze of a tigress.

Starke looked away, down at himself. There was blood on his kilt, a brown smear of it across his chest. It was not his blood. He drew the knife slowly out of its sheath. The blade was dull and crusted, still a little wet.

Starke looked at Beudag. His lips were stiff, swollen. He moistened them and said hoarsely, "What happened?"

She shook her head, slowly, not speaking. Her eyes did not waver.

A black, cold rage took hold of Starke and shook him. Rann! He rose and went forward, letting the sweep go where it would. He began to untie Beudag's wrists.

A shape swam toward them out of the red mist. A longship with two heavy sweeps bursting fire astern and a slender figurehead shaped like a woman. A woman with hair and eyes of aquamarine. It came alongside the skiff.

A rope ladder snaked down. Men lined the low rail. Slender men with skin that glistened white like powdered snow, and hair the color of distant shallows.

33

One of them said, "Come aboard, Hugh Starke."

Starke went back to the sweep. It bit into the sea, sending the skiff in a swift arc away from Rann's ship.

Grapnels flew, hooking the skiff at thwart and gunwale. Bows appeared in the hands of the men, wicked curving things with barbed metal shafts on the string. The man said again, politely, "Come aboard."

Hugh Starke finished untying Beudag. He didn't speak. There seemed to be nothing to say. He stood back while she climbed the ladder and then followed. The skiff was cast loose. The longship veered away, gathering speed.

Starke said, "Where are we going?"

The man smiled. "To Falga."

Starke nodded. He went below with Beudag into a cabin with soft couches covered with spider-silk and panels of dark wood beautifully painted, dim fantastic scenes from the past of Rann's people. They sat opposite each other. They still did not speak.

*

They raised Falga in the opal dawn—a citadel of basalt cliffs rising sheer from the burning sea, with a long arm holding a harbor full of ships. There were green fields inland, and beyond, cloaked in the eternal mists of Venus, the Mountains of White Clouds lifted spaceward. Starke wished that he had never seen the Mountains of White Cloud. Then, looking at his hands, lean and strong on his long thighs, he wasn't so sure. He thought of Rann waiting for him. Anger, excitement, a confused violence of emotion set him pacing nervously.

Beudag sat quietly, withdrawn, waiting.

The longship threaded the crowded moorings and slid into place alongside a stone quay. Men rushed to make fast. They were human men, as Starke judged humans, like Beudag and himself. They had the shimmering silver hair and fair skin of the plateau peoples, the fine-cut faces and straight bodies. They wore leather collars with metal tags and they went naked like beasts, and they were gaunt and bowed with labor. Here and there a man with pale blue-green hair and resplendent harness stood godlike above the swarming masses.

Starke and Beudag went ashore. They might have been prisoners or honored guests, surrounded by their escort from the ship. Streets ran back from the harbor, twisting and climbing crazily up the cliffs. Houses climbed on each others backs. It had begun to rain, the heavy steaming downpour of Venus, and the moist heat brought out the choking stench of people, too many people.

They climbed, ankle deep in water sweeping down the streets that were half stairway. Thin naked children peered out of the houses, out of narrow alleys. Twice they passed through market squares where women with the blank faces of defeat drew back from stalls of coarse food to let the party through.

There was something wrong. After a while Starke realized it was the silence. In all that horde of humanity no one laughed, or sang, or shouted. Even the children never spoke above a whisper. Starke began to feel a little sick. Their eyes had a look in them....

He glanced at Beudag, and away again.

The waterfront streets ended in a sheer basalt face honeycombed with galleries. Starke's party entered them, still climbing. They passed level after level of huge caverns, open to the sea. There was the same crowding, the same stench, the same silence. Eyes glinted in the half-light, bare feet moved furtively on stone. Somewhere a baby cried thinly, and was hushed at once.

They came out on the cliff top, into the clean high air. There was a city here. Broad streets, lined with trees, low rambling villas of the

35

black rock set in walled gardens, drowned in brilliant vines and giant ferns and flowers. Naked men and women worked in the gardens, or hauled carts of rubbish through the alleys, or hurried on errands, slipping furtively across the main streets where they intersected the mews.

The party turned away from the sea, heading toward an ebon palace that sat like a crown above the city. The steaming rain beat on Starke's bare body, and up here you could get the smell of the rain, even through the heavy perfume of the flowers. You could smell Venus in the rain—musky and primitive and savagely alive, a fecund giantess with passion flowers in her outstretched hands. Starke set his feet down like a panther and his eyes burned a smoky amber.

They entered the palace of Rann....

She received them in the same apartment where Starke had come to after the crash. Through a broad archway he could see the high bed where his old body had lain before the life went out of it. The red sea steamed under the rain outside, the rusty fog coiling languidly through the open arches of the gallery. Rann watched them lazily from a raised couch set massively into the wall. Her long sparkling legs sprawled arrogantly across the black spider-silk draperies. This time her tabard was a pale yellow. Her eyes were still the color of shoal-water, still amused, still secret, still dangerous.

Starke said, "So you made me do it after all."

"And you're angry." She laughed, her teeth showing white and pointed as bone needles. Her gaze held Starke's. There was nothing casual about it. Starke's hawk eyes turned molten yellow, like hot gold, and did not waver.

Beudag stood like a bronze spear, her forearms crossed beneath her bare sharp breasts. Two of Rann's palace guards stood behind her.

Starke began to walk toward Rann.

She watched him come. She let him get close enough to reach out and touch her, and then she said slyly, "It's a good body, isn't it?"

*

Starke looked at her for a moment. Then he laughed. He threw back his head and roared, and struck the great corded muscles of his belly with his fist. Presently he looked straight into Rann's eyes and said:

"I know you."

She nodded. "We know each other. Sit down, Hugh Starke." She swung her long legs over to make room, half erect now, looking at Beudag. Starke sat down. He did not look at Beudag.

Rann said, "Will your people surrender now?"

Beudag did not move, not even her eyelids. "If Faolan is dead—yes."

"And if he's not?"

Beudag stiffened. Starke did too.

"Then," said Beudag quietly, "they'll wait."

"Until he is?"

"Or until they must surrender."

Rann nodded. To the guards she said, "See that this woman is well fed and well treated."

Beudag and her escort had turned to go when Starke said, "Wait." The guards looked at Rann, who nodded, and glanced quizzically at Starke. Starke said:

"Is Faolan dead?"

Rann hesitated. Then she smiled. "No. You have the most damnably tough mind, Starke. You struck deep, but not deep enough. He may still die, but.... No, he's not dead." She turned to Beudag and said with easy mockery, "You needn't hold anger against Starke. I'm the one who should be angry." Her eyes came back to Starke. They didn't look angry.

Starke said, "There's something else. Conan—the Conan that used to be, before Falga."

"Beudag's Conan."

"Yeah. Why did he betray his people?"

Rann studied him. Her strange pale lips curved, her sharp white teeth glistening wickedly with barbed humor. Then she turned to Beudag. Beudag was still standing like a carved image, but her smooth muscles were ridged with tension, and her eyes were not the eyes of an image.

"Conan or Starke," said Rann, "she's still Beudag, isn't she? All right, I'll tell you. Conan betrayed his people because I put it into his mind to do it. He fought me. He made a good fight of it. But he wasn't quite as tough as you are, Starke."

There was a silence. For the first time since entering the room, Hugh Starke looked at Beudag. After a moment she sighed and lifted her chin and smiled, a deep, faint smile. The guards walked out beside her, but she was more erect and lighter of step than either of them.

"Well," said Rann, when they were gone, "and what about you, Hugh-Starke-Called-Conan."

"Have I any choice?"

"I always keep my bargains."

"Then give me my dough and let me clear the hell out of here."

"Sure that's what you want?"

"That's what I want."

"You could stay a while, you know."

"With you."

Rann lifted her frosty-white shoulders. "I'm not promising half my kingdom, or even part of it. But you might be amused."

"I got no sense of humor."

"Don't you even want to see what happens to Crom Dhu?"

Starke got up. He said savagely, "The hell with Crom Dhu."

"And Beudag."

"And Beudag." He stopped, then fixed Rann with uncompromising yellow eyes. "No. Not Beudag. What are you going to do to her?"

"Nothing."

"Don't give me that."

"I say again, nothing. Whatever is done, her own people will do."

"What do you mean?"

"I mean that little Dagger-in-the-Sheath will be rested, cared for, and fattened, for a few days. Then I shall take her aboard my own ship and join the fleet before Crom Dhu. Beudag will be made quite comfortable at the masthead, where her people can see her plainly. She will stay there until the Rock surrenders. It depends on her own people how long she stays. She'll be given water. Not much, but enough."

Starke stared at her. He stared at her a long time. Then he spat deliberately on the floor and said in a perfectly flat voice: "How soon can I get out of here?"

Rann laughed, a small casual chuckle. "Humans," she said, "are so damned queer. I don't think I'll ever understand them." She reached out and struck a gong that stood in a carved frame beside the couch. The soft deep shimmering note had a sad quality of nostalgia. Rann lay back against the silken cushions and sighed.

"Goodbye, Hugh Starke."

A pause. Then, regretfully:

"Goodbye—Conan!"

*

They had made good time along the rim of the Red Sea. One of Rann's galleys had taken them to the edge of the Southern Ocean and left them on a narrow shingle beach under the cliffs. From there they had climbed to the rimrock and gone on foot—Hugh-Starke-Called-Conan and four of Rann's arrogant shining men. They were supposed to be guide and escort. They were courteous, and they kept pace uncomplainingly though Starke marched as though the devil were pricking his heels. But they were armed, and Starke was not.

Sometimes, very faintly, Starke was aware of Rann's mind touching his with the velvet delicacy of a cat's paw. Sometimes he started out of his sleep with her image sharp in his mind, her lips touched with the mocking, secret smile. He didn't like that. He didn't like it at all.

But he liked even less the picture that stayed with him waking or sleeping. The picture he wouldn't look at. The picture of a tall woman with hair like loose fire on her neck, walking on light proud feet between her guards.

She'll be given water, Rann said. Not much, but enough.

Starke gripped the solid squareness of the box that held his million credits and set the miles reeling backward from under his sandals.

On the fifth night one of Rann's men spoke quietly across the campfire. "Tomorrow," he said, "we'll reach the pass."

Starke got up and went away by himself, to the edge of the rimrock that fell sheer to the burning sea. He sat down. The red fog wrapped him like a mist of blood. He thought of the blood on Beudag's breast the first time he saw her. He thought of the blood on his knife, crusted and dried. He thought of the blood poured rank and smoking into the gutters of Crom Dhu. The fog has to be red, he thought. Of all the goddam colors in the universe, it has to be red. Red like Beudag's hair.

He held out his hands and looked at them, because he could still feel the silken warmth of that hair against his skin. There was nothing there now but the old white scars of another man's battles.

He set his fists against his temples and wished for his old body back again—the little stunted abortion that had clawed and scratched its way to survival through sheer force of mind. A most damnably tough mind, Rann had said. Yeah. It had had to be tough. But a mind was a mind. It didn't have emotions. It just figured out something coldly and then went ahead and never questioned, and it controlled the body utterly, because the body was only the worthless machinery that carried the mind around. Worthless. Yeah. The few women he'd ever looked at had told him that—and he hadn't even minded much. The old body hadn't given him any trouble.

He was having trouble now.

Starke got up and walked.

Tomorrow we reach the pass.

Tomorrow we go away from the Red Sea. There are nine planets and the whole damn Belt. There are women on all of them. All shapes, colors, and sizes, human, semi-human, and God knows what. With a million credits a guy could buy half of them, and with Conan's body he could buy the rest. What's a woman, anyway? Only a....

*Water. She'll be given water. Not much, but enough.*

Conan reached out and took hold of a spire of rock, and his muscles stood out like knotted ropes. "Oh God," he whispered, "what's the matter with me?"

"*Love.*"

It wasn't God who answered. It was Rann. He saw her plainly in his mind, heard her voice like a silver bell.

"Conan was a man, Hugh Starke. He was whole, body and heart and brain. He knew how to love, and with him it wasn't women, but one woman—and her name was Beudag. I broke him, but it wasn't easy. I can't break you."

41

# LORELEI OF THE RED MIST

Starke stood for a long, long time. He did not move, except that he trembled. Then he took from his belt the box containing his million credits and threw it out as far as he could over the cliff edge. The red mist swallowed it up. He did not hear it strike the surface of the sea. Perhaps in that sea there was no splashing. He did not wait to find out.

He turned back along the rimrock, toward a place where he remembered a cleft, or chimney, leading down. And the four shining men who wore Rann's harness came silently out of the heavy luminous night and ringed him in. Their sword-points caught sharp red glimmers from the sky.

Starke had nothing on him but a kilt and sandals, and a cloak of tight-woven spider-silk that shed the rain.

"Rann sent you?" he said.

The men nodded.

"To kill me?"

Again they nodded. The blood drained out of Starke's face, leaving it grey and stony under the bronze. His hand went to his throat, over the gold fastening of his cloak.

The four men closed in like dancers.

*

Starke loosed his cloak and swung it like a whip across their faces. It confused them for a second, for a heartbeat—no more, but long enough. Starke left two of them to tangle their blades in the heavy fabric and leaped aside. A sharp edge slipped and turned along his ribs, and then he had reached in low and caught a man around the ankles, and used the thrashing body for a flail.

The body was strangely light, as though the bones in it were no more than rigid membrane, like a fish.

If he had stayed to fight, they would have finished him in seconds. They were fighting men, and quick. But Starke didn't stay. He gained his moment's grace and used it. They were hard on his heels, their points all but pricking his back as he ran, but he made it. Along the rimrock, out along a narrow tongue that jutted over the sea, and then outward, far outward, into red fog and dim fire that rolled around his plummeting body.

Oh God, he thought, if I guessed wrong and there *is* a beach....

The breath tore out of his lungs. His ears cracked, went dead. He held his arms out beyond his head, the thumbs locked together, his neck braced forward against the terrific upward push. He struck the surface of the sea.

There was no splash.

Dim coiling fire that drifted with infinite laziness around him, caressing his body with slow, tingling sparks. A feeling of lightness, as though his flesh had become one with the drifting fire. A sense of suffocation that had no basis in fact and gave way gradually to a strange exhilaration. There was no shock of impact, no crushing pressure. Merely a cushioning softness, like dropping into a bed of compressed air. Starke felt himself turning end over end, pinwheel fashion, and then that stopped, so that he sank quietly and without haste to the bottom.

Or rather, into the crystalline upper reaches of what seemed to be a forest.

He could see it spreading away along the downward-sloping floor of the ocean, into the vague red shadows of distance. Slender fantastic trunks upholding a maze of delicate shining branches, without leaves or fruit. They were like trees exquisitely molded from ice, transparent, holding the lambent shifting fire of the strange sea. Starke didn't think they were, or ever had been, alive. More like coral, he thought, or some vagary of mineral deposit. Beautiful, though. Like something you'd see in a dream. Beautiful, silent, and somehow deadly.

He couldn't explain that feeling of deadliness. Nothing moved in the red drifts between the trunks. It was nothing about the trees themselves. It was just something he sensed.

He began to move among the upper branches, following the downward drop of the slope.

He found that he could swim quite easily. Or perhaps it was more like flying. The dense gas buoyed him up, almost balancing the weight of his body, so that it was easy to swoop along, catching a crystal branch and using it as a lever to throw himself forward to the next one.

He went deeper and deeper into the heart of the forbidden Southern Ocean. Nothing stirred. The fairy forest stretched limitless ahead. And Starke was afraid.

Rann came into his mind abruptly. Her face, clearly outlined, was full of mockery.

"I'm going to watch you die, Hugh-Starke-Called-Conan. But before you die, I'll show you something. Look."

Her face dimmed, and in its place was Crom Dhu rising bleak into the red fog, the longships broken and sunk in the harbor, and Rann's fleet around it in a shining circle.

One ship in particular. The flagship. The vision in Starke's mind rushed toward it, narrowed down to the masthead platform. To the woman who stood there, naked, erect, her body lashed tight with thin cruel cords.

A woman with red hair blowing in the slow wind, and blue eyes that looked straight ahead like a falcon's, at Crom Dhu.

Beudag.

Rann's laughter ran across the picture and blurred it like a ripple of ice-cold water.

"You'd have done better," she said, "to take the clean steel when I offered it to you."

She was gone, and Starke's mind was as empty and cold as the mind of a corpse. He found that he was standing still, clinging to a branch, his face upturned as though by some blind instinct, his sight blurred.

He had never cried before in all his life, nor prayed.

There was no such thing as time, down there in the smoky shadows of the sea bottom. It might have been minutes or hours later that Hugh Starke discovered he was being hunted.

\*

There were three of them, slipping easily among the shining branches. They were pale golden, almost phosphorescent, about the size of large hounds. Their eyes were huge, jewel-like in their slim sharp faces. They possessed four members that might have been legs and arms, retracted now against their arrowing bodies. Golden membranes spread wing-like from head to flank, and they moved like wings, balancing expertly the thrust of the flat, powerful tails.

They could have closed in on him easily, but they didn't seem to be in any hurry. Starke had sense enough not to wear himself out trying to get away. He kept on going, watching them. He discovered that the crystal branches could be broken, and he selected himself one with a sharp forked tip, shoving it swordwise under his belt. He didn't suppose it would do much good, but it made him feel better.

He wondered why the things didn't jump him and get it over with. They looked hungry enough, the way they were showing him their teeth. But they kept about the same distance away, in a sort of crescent formation, and every so often the ones on the outside would make a tentative dart at him, then fall back as he swerved away. It wasn't like being hunted so much as....

Starke's eyes narrowed. He began suddenly to feel much more afraid than he had before, and he wouldn't have believed that possible.

The things weren't hunting him at all. They were herding him.

There was nothing he could do about it. He tried stopping, and they swooped in and snapped at him, working expertly together so that while he was trying to stab one of them with his clumsy weapon, the others were worrying his heels like sheepdogs at a recalcitrant wether.

Starke, like the wether, bowed to the inevitable and went where he was driven. The golden hounds showed their teeth in animal laughter and sniffed hungrily at the thread of blood he left behind him in the slow red coils of fire.

After a while he heard the music.

It seemed to be some sort of a harp, with a strange quality of vibration in the notes. It wasn't like anything he'd ever heard before. Perhaps the gas of which the sea was composed was an extraordinarily good conductor of sound, with a property of diffusion that made the music seem to come from everywhere at once—softly at first, like something touched upon in a dream, and then, as he drew closer to the source, swelling into a racing, rippling flood of melody that wrapped itself around his nerves with a demoniac shiver of ecstasy.

The golden hounds began to fret with excitement, spreading their shining wings, driving him impatiently faster through the crystal branches.

Starke could feel the vibration growing in him—the very fibres of his muscles shuddering in sympathy with the unearthly harp. He guessed there was a lot of the music he couldn't hear. Too high, too low for his ears to register. But he could feel it.

He began to go faster, not because of the hounds, but because he wanted to. The deep quivering in his flesh excited him. He began to breathe harder, partly because of increased exertion, and some chemical quality of the mixture he breathed made him slightly drunk.

The thrumming harp-song stroked and stung him, waking a deeper, darker music, and suddenly he saw Beudag clearly—half-veiled and mystic in the candle light at Faolan's dun; smooth curving bronze, her hair loose fire about her throat. A great stab of agony went through him. He called her name, once, and the harp-song swept it up and away, and then suddenly there was no music any more, and no forest, and nothing but cold embers in Starke's heart.

He could see everything quite clearly in the time it took him to float from the top of the last tree to the floor of the plain. He had no idea how long a time that was. It didn't matter. It was one of those moments when time doesn't have any meaning.

The rim of the forest fell away in a long curve that melted glistening into the spark-shot sea. From it the plain stretched out, a level glassy floor of black obsidian, the spew of some long-dead volcano. Or was it dead? It seemed to Starke that the light here was redder, more vital, as though he were close to the source from which it sprang.

As he looked farther over the plain, the light seemed to coalesce into a shimmering curtain that wavered like the heat veils that dance along the Mercurian Twilight Belt at high noon. For one brief instant he glimpsed a picture on the curtain—a city, black, shining, fantastically turreted, the gigantic reflection of a Titan's dream. Then it was gone, and the immediate menace of the foreground took all of Starke's attention.

\*

# LORELEI OF THE RED mIST

He saw the flock, herded by more of the golden hounds. And he saw the shepherd, with the harp held silent between his hands.

The flock moved sluggishly, phosphorescently.

One hundred, two hundred silent, limply floating warriors drifting down the red dimness. In pairs, singly, or in pallid clusters they came. The golden hounds winged silently, leisurely around them, channeling them in tides that sluiced toward the fantastic ebon city.

The shepherd stood, a crop of obsidian, turning his shark-pale face. His sharp, aquamarine eyes found Starke. His silvery hand leapt beckoning over hard-threads, striking them a blow. Reverberations ran out, seized Starke, shook him. He dropped his crystal dagger.

Hot screens of fire exploded in his eyes, bubbles whirled and danced in his eardrums. He lost all muscular control. His dark head fell forward against the thick blackness of hair on his chest; his golden eyes dissolved into weak, inane yellow, and his mouth loosened. He wanted to fight, but it was useless. This shepherd was one of the sea-people he had come to see, and one way or another he would see him.

Dark blood filled his aching eyes. He felt himself led, nudged, forced first this way, then that. A golden hound slipped by, gave him a pressure which roiled him over into a current of sea-blood. It ran down past where the shepherd stood with only a harp for a weapon.

Starke wondered dimly whether these other warriors in the flock, drifting, were dead or alive like himself. He had another surprise coming.

They were all Rann's men. Men of Falga. Silver men with burning green hair. Rann's men. One of them, a huge warrior colored like powdered salt, wandered aimlessly by on another tide, his green eyes dull. He looked dead.

What business had the sea-people with the dead warriors of Falga? Why the hounds and the shepherd's harp? Questions eddied like lifted silt in Starke's tired, hanging head. Eddied and settled flat.

Starke joined the pilgrimage.

The hounds with deft flickerings of wings, ushered him into the midst of the flock. Bodies brushed against him. *Cold* bodies. He wanted to cry out. The cords of his neck constricted. In his mind the cry went forward:

"Are you alive, men of Falga?"

No answer; but the drift of scarred, pale bodies. The eyes in them knew nothing. They had forgotten Falga. They had forgotten Rann for whom they had lifted blade. Their tongues lolling in mouths asked nothing but sleep. They were getting it.

A hundred, two hundred strong they made a strange human river slipping toward the gigantic city wall. Starke-called-Conan and his bitter enemies going together. From the corners of his eyes, Starke saw the shepherd move. The shepherd was like Rann and her people who had years ago abandoned the sea to live on land. The shepherd seemed colder, more fish-like, though. There were small translucent webs between the thin fingers and spanning the long-toed feet. Thin, scar-like gills in the shadow of his tapered chin, lifted and sealed in the current, eating, taking sustenance from the blood-colored sea.

The harp spoke and the golden hounds obeyed. The harp spoke and the bodies twisted uneasily, as in a troubled sleep. A triple chord of it came straight at Starke. His fingers clenched.

"—and the dead shall walk again—"

Another ironic ripple of music.

"—and Rann's men will rise again, this time against her—"

Starke had time to feel a brief, bewildered shivering, before the current hurled him forward. Clamoring drunkenly, witlessly, all about him, the dead, muscleless warriors of Falga, tried to crush past him, all of them at once....

Long ago some vast sea Titan had dreamed of avenues struck from black stone. Each stone the size of three men tall. There had been a dream of walls going up and up until they dissolved into scarlet mist. There had been another dream of sea-gardens in which fish hung like erotic flowers, on tendrils of sensitive film-tissue. Whole beds of fish clung to garden base, like colonies of flowers aglow with sunlight. And on occasion a black amoebic presence filtered by, playing the gardener, weeding out an amber flower here, an amythystine bloom there.

And the sea Titan had dreamed of endless balustrades and battlements, of windowless turrets where creatures swayed like radium-skinned phantoms, carrying their green plumes of hair in their lifted palms and looked down with curious, insolent eyes from on high. Women with shimmering bodies like some incredible coral harvested and kept high over these black stone streets, each in its archway.

Starke was alone. Falga's warriors had gone off along a dim subterranean vent, vanished. Now the faint beckoning of harp and the golden hounds behind him, turned him down a passage that opened out into a large circular stone room, one end of which opened out into a hall. Around the ebon ceiling, slender schools of fish swam. It was their bright effulgence that gave light to the room. They had been there, breeding, eating, dying, a thousand years, giving light to the place, and they would be there, breeding and dying, a thousand more.

The harp faded until it was only a murmur.

Starke found his feet. Strength returned to him. He was able to see the man in the center of the room well. Too well.

# LEIGH BRACKETT AND RAY BRADBURY

The man hung in the fire tide. Chains of wrought bronze held his thin fleshless ankles so he couldn't escape. His body desired it. It floated up.

It had been dead a long time. It was gaseous with decomposition and it wanted to rise to the surface of the Red Sea. The chains prevented this. Its arms weaved like white scarves before a sunken white face. Black hair trembled on end.

*

He was one of Faolan's men. One of the Rovers. One of those who had gone down at Falga because of Conan.

His name was Geil.

Starke remembered.

The part of him that was Conan remembered the name.

The dead lips moved.

"Conan. What luck is this! Conan. I make you welcome."

The words were cruel, the lips around them loose and dead. It seemed to Starke an anger and embittered wrath lay deep in those hollow eyes. The lips twitched again.

"I went down at Falga for you and Rann, Conan. Remember?"

Part of Starke remembered and twisted in agony.

"We're all here, Conan. All of us. Clev and Mannt and Bron and Aesur. Remember Aesur, who could shape metal over his spine, prying it with his fingers? Aesur is here, big as a sea-monster, waiting in a niche, cold and loose as string. The sea-shepherds collected us. Collected us for a purpose of irony. Look!"

The boneless fingers hung out, as in a wind, pointing.

Starke turned slowly, and his heart pounded an uneven, shattering drum beat. His jaw clinched and his eyes blurred. That part of him that was Conan cried out. Conan was so much of him and he so much of Conan it was impossible for a cleavage. They'd grown

51

together like pearl material around sand-specule, layer on layer. Starke cried out.

In the hall which this circular room overlooked, stood a thousand men.

In lines of fifty across, shoulder to shoulder, the men of Crom Dhu stared unseeingly up at Starke. Here and there a face became shockingly familiar. Old memory cried their names.

"Bron! Clev! Mannt! Aesur!"

The collected decomposition of their bodily fluids raised them, drifted them above the flaggings. Each of them was chained, like Geil.

Geil whispered. "We have made a union with the men of Falga!"

Starke pulled back.

"Falga!"

"In death, all men are equals." He took his time with it. He was in no hurry. Dead bodies under-sea are never in a hurry. They sort of bump and drift and bide their time. "The dead serve those who give them a semblance of life. Tomorrow we march against Crom Dhu."

"You're crazy! Crom Dhu is *your* home! It's the place of Beudag and Faolan—"

"And—" interrupted the hanging corpse, quietly, "Conan? Eh?" He laughed. A crystal dribble of bubbles ran up from the slack mouth. "Especially Conan. Conan who sank us at Falga...."

Starke moved swiftly. Nobody stopped him. He had the corpse's short blade in an instant. Geil's chest made a cold, silent sheathe for it. The blade went like a fork through butter.

Coldly, without noticing this, Geil's voice spoke out:

"Stab me, cut me. You can't kill me any deader. Make sections of me. Play butcher. A flank, a hand, a heart! And while you're at it, I'll tell you the plan."

Snarling, Starke seized the blade out again. With blind violence he gave sharp blow after blow at the body, cursing bitterly, and the body took each blow, rocking in the red tide a little, and said with a matter-of-fact tone:

"We'll march out of the sea to Crom Dhu's gates. Romna and the others, looking down, recognizing us, will have the gates thrown wide to welcome us." The head tilted lazily, the lips peeled wide and folded down languidly over the words. "Think of the elation, Conan! The moment when Bron and Mannt and Aesur and I and yourself, yes, even yourself, Conan, return to Crom Dhu!"

*

Starke saw it, vividly. Saw it like a tapestry woven for him. He stood back, gasping for breath, his nostrils flaring, seeing what his blade had done to Geil's body, and seeing the great stone gates of Crom Dhu crashing open. The deliberation. The happiness, the elation to Faolan and Romna to see old friends returned. Old Rovers, long thought dead. Alive again, come to help! It made a picture!

With great deliberation, Starke struck flat across before him.

Geil's head, severed from its lazy body, began, with infinite tiredness, to float toward the ceiling. As it traveled upward, now facing, now bobbling the back of its skull toward Starke, it finished its nightmare speaking:

"And then, once inside the gates, what then, Conan? Can you guess? Can you guess what we'll do, Conan?"

Starke stared at nothingness, the sword trembling in his fist. From far away he heard Geil's voice:

"—we will kill Faolan in his hall. He will die with surprised lips. Romna's harp will lie in his disemboweled stomach. His heart with its last pulsings will sound the strings. And as for Beudag—"

Starke tried to push the thoughts away, raging and helpless. Geil's body was no longer anything to look at. He had done all he could to it. Starke's face was bleached white and scraped down to the insane bone of it, "You'd kill your own people!"

Geil's separated head lingered at the ceiling, light-fish illuminating its ghastly features. "Our people? But we have no people! We're another race now. The dead. We do the biddings of the sea-shepherds."

Starke looked out into the hall, then he looked at the circular wall.

"Okay," he said, without tone in his voice. "Come out. Where ever you're hiding and using this voice-throwing act. Come on out and talk straight."

In answer, an entire section of ebon stones fell back on silent hingework. Starke saw a long slender black marble table. Six people sat behind it in carven midnight thrones.

They were all men. Naked except for film-like garments about their loins. They looked at Starke with no particular hatred or curiosity. One of them cradled a harp. It was the shepherd who'd drawn Starke through the gate. Amusedly, his webbed fingers lay on the strings, now and then bringing out a clear sound from one of the two hundred strands.

The shepherd stopped Starke's rush forward with a cry of that harp!

The blade in his hand was red hot. He dropped it.

The shepherd put a head on the story. "And then? And then we will march Rann's dead warriors all the way to Falga. There, Rann's people, seeing the warriors, will be overjoyed, hysterical to find their friends and relatives returned. They, too, will fling wide Falga's defenses. And death will walk in, disguised as resurrection."

Starke nodded, slowly, wiping his hand across his cheek. "Back on Earth we call that psychology. *Good* psychology. But will it fool Rann?"

"Rann will be with her ships at Crom Dhu. While she's gone, the innocent population will let in their lost warriors gladly." The shepherd had amused green eyes. He looked like a youth of some seventeen years. Deceptively young. If Starke guessed right, the youth was nearer to two centuries old. That's how you lived and looked when you were under the Red Sea. Something about the emanations of it kept part of you young.

Starke lidded his yellow hawks' eyes thoughtfully. "You've got all aces. You'll win. But what's Crom Dhu to you? Why not just Rann? She's one of you, you hate her more than you do the Rovers. Her ancestors came up on land, you never got over hating them for that—"

The shepherd shrugged. "Toward Crom Dhu we have little actual hatred. Except that they are by nature land-men, even if they do rove by boat, and pillagers. One day they might try their luck on the sunken devices of this city."

Starke put a hand out. "We're fighting Rann, too. Don't forget, we're on your side!"

"Whereas we are on no one's," retorted the green-haired youth, "Except our own. Welcome to the army which will attack Crom Dhu."

"Me! By the gods, over my dead body!"

"That," said the youth, amusedly, "is what we intend. We've worked many years, you see, to perfect the plan. We're not much good out on land. We needed bodies that could do the work for us. So, every time Faolan lost a ship or Rann lost a ship, we were there, with our golden hounds, waiting. Collecting. Saving. Waiting until we had enough of each side's warriors. They'll do the fighting for us.

Oh, not for long, of course. The Source energy will give them a semblance of life, a momentary electrical ability of walk and combat, but once out of water they'll last only half an hour. But that should be time enough once the gates of Crom Dhu and Falga are open."

\*

Starke said, "Rann will find some way around you. Get her first. Attack Crom Dhu the following day."

The youth deliberated. "You're stalling. But there's sense in it. Rann is most important. We'll get Falga first, then. You'll have a bit of time in which to raise false hopes."

Starke began to get sick again. The room swam.

Very quietly, very easily, Rann came into his mind again. He felt her glide in like the merest touch of a sea fern weaving in a tide pool.

He closed his mind down, but not before she snatched at a shred of thought. Her aquamarine eyes reflected desire and inquiry.

"Hugh Starke, you're with the sea people?"

Her voice was soft. He shook his head.

"Tell me, Hugh Starke. How are you plotting against Falga?"

He said nothing. He thought nothing. He shut his eyes.

Her fingernails glittered, raking at his mind. "Tell me!"

His thoughts rolled tightly into a metal sphere which nothing could dent.

Rann laughed unpleasantly and leaned forward until she filled every dark horizon of his skull with her shimmering body. "All right. I *gave* you Conan's body. Now I'll take it away."

She struck him a combined blow of her eyes, her writhing lips, her bone-sharp teeth. "Go back to your old body, go back to your old body, Hugh Starke," she hissed. "Go back! Leave Conan to his idiocy. Go back to your old body!"

Fear had him. He fell down upon his face, quivering and jerking. You could fight a man with a sword. But how could you fight this thing in your brain? He began to suck sobbing breaths through his lips. He was screaming. He could not hear himself. Her voice rushed in from the dim outer red universe, destroying him.

"Hugh Starke! Go back to your old body!"

His old body was—dead!

And she was sending him back into it.

Part of him shot endwise through red fog.

He lay on a mountain plateau overlooking the harbor of Falga.

Red fog coiled and snaked around him. Flame birds dived eerily down at his staring, blind eyes.

His old body held him.

Putrefaction stuffed his nostrils. The flesh sagged and slipped greasily on his loosened structure. He felt small again and ugly. Flame birds nibbled, picking, choosing between his ribs. Pain gorged him. Cold, blackness, nothingness filled him. Back in his old body. Forever.

He didn't want that.

The plateau, the red fog vanished. The flame birds, too.

He lay once more on the floor of the sea shepherds, struggling.

"That was just a start," Rann told him. "Next time, I'll leave you up there on the plateau in that body. *Now*, will you tell the plans of the sea people? And go on living in Conan? He's yours, if you tell." She smirked. "You don't want to be dead."

Starke tried to reason it out. Any way he turned was the wrong way. He grunted out a breath. "If I tell, you'll still kill Beudag."

"Her life in exchange for what you know, Hugh Starke."

Her answer was too swift. It had the sound of treachery. Starke did not believe. He would die. That would solve it. Then, at least, Rann would die when the sea people carried out their strategy. That much revenge, at least, damn it.

Then he got the idea.

He coughed out a laugh, raised his weak head to look at the startled sea shepherd. His little dialogue with Rann had taken about ten seconds, actually, but it had seemed a century. The sea shepherd stepped forward.

Starke tried to get to his feet. "Got—got a proposition for you. You with the harp. Rann's inside me. *Now.* Unless you guarantee Crom Dhu and Beudag's safety, I'll tell her some things she might want to be in on!"

The sea shepherd drew a knife.

Starke shook his head, coldly. "Put it away. Even if you get me I'll give the whole damned strategy to Rann."

The shepherd dropped his hand. He was no fool.

Rann tore at Starke's brain. "Tell me! Tell me their plan!"

He felt like a guy in a revolving door. Starke got the sea men in focus. He saw that they were afraid now, doubtful and nervous. "I'll be dead in a minute," said Starke. "Promise me the safety of Crom Dhu and I'll die without telling Rann a thing."

The sea shepherd hesitated, then raised his palm upward. "I promise," he said. "Crom Dhu will go untouched."

Starke sighed. He let his head fall forward until it hit the floor. Then he rolled over, put his hands over his eyes. "It's a deal. Go give Rann hell for me, will you, boys? Give her hell!"

As he drifted into mind darkness, Rann waited for him. Feebly, he told her. "Okay, duchess. You'd kill me even if I'd told you the idea. I'm ready. Try your god-awfullest to shove me back into that stinking body of mine. I'll fight you all the way there!"

Rann screamed. It was a pretty frustrated scream. Then the pains began. She did a lot of work on his mind in the next minute.

That part of him that was Conan held on like a clam holding to its precious contents.

The odor of putrid flesh returned. The blood mist returned. The flame birds fell down at him in spirals of sparks and blistering smoke, to winnow his naked ribs.

Starke spoke one last word before the blackness took him.

"Beudag."

*

He never expected to awaken again.

He awoke just the same.

There was red sea all around him. He lay on a kind of stone bed, and the young sea shepherd sat beside him, looking down at him, smiling delicately.

Starke did not dare move for a while. He was afraid his head might fall off and whirl away like a big fish, using its ears as propellers. "Lord," he muttered, barely turning his head.

The sea creature stirred. "You won. You fought Rann, and won."

Starke groaned. "I feel like something passed through a wild-cat's intestines. She's gone. Rann's gone." He laughed. "That makes me sad. Somebody cheer me up. Rann's gone." He felt of his big, flat-muscled body. "She was bluffing. Trying to drive me batty. She knew she couldn't really tuck me back into that carcass, but she didn't want me to know. It was like a baby's nightmare before it's born. Or maybe you haven't got a memory like me." He rolled over, stretching. "She won't ever get in my head again. I've locked the gate and swallowed the key." His eyes dilated. "What's *your* name?"

"Linnl," said the man with the harp. "You didn't tell Rann our strategy?"

"What do *you* think?"

Linnl smiled sincerely. "I think I like you, man of Crom Dhu. I think I like your hatred for Rann. I think I like the way you handled the entire matter, wanted to kill Rann and save Crom Dhu, and being so willing to die to accomplish either."

"That's a lot of thinking. Yeah, and what about that promise you made?"

"It will be kept."

Starke gave him a hand. "Linnl, you're okay. If I ever get back to Earth, so help me, I'll never bait a hook again and drop it in the sea." It was lost to Linnl. Starke forgot it, and went on, laughing. There was an edge of hysteria to it. Relief. You got booted around for days, people milled in and out of your mind like it was a bargain basement counter, pawing over the treads and convolutions, yelling and fighting; the woman you loved was starved on a ship masthead, and as a climax a lady with green eyes tried to make you a filling for an accident-mangled body. And now you had an ally.

And you couldn't believe it.

He laughed in little starts and stops, his eyes shut.

"Will you let me take care of Rann when the time comes?"

His fingers groped hungrily upward, closed on an imaginary figure of her, pressed, tightened, choked.

Linnl said, "She's yours. I'd like the pleasure, but you have as much if not more of a revenge to take. Come along. We start now. You've been asleep for one entire period."

Starke let himself down gingerly. He didn't want to break a leg off. He felt if someone touched him he might disintegrate.

He managed to let the tide handle him, do all the work. He swam carefully after Linnl down three passageways where an occasional silver inhabitant of the city slid by.

# LEIGH BRACKETT AND RAY BRADBURY

Drifting below them in a vast square hall, each gravitating but imprisoned by leg-shackles, the warriors of Falga looked up with pale cold eyes at Starke and Linnl. Occasional discharges of light-fish from interstices in the walls, passed luminous, fleeting glows over the warriors. The light-fish flirted briefly in a long shining rope that tied knots around the dead faces and as quickly untied them. Then the light-fish pulsed away and the red color of the sea took over.

Bathed in wine, thought Starke, without humor. He leaned forward.

"Men of Falga!"

Linnl plucked a series of harp-threads.

"Aye." A deep suggestion of sound issued from a thousand dead lips.

"We go to sack Rann's citadel!"

"Rann!" came the muffled thunder of voices.

At the sound of another tune, the golden hounds appeared. They touched the chains. The men of Falga, released, danced through the red sea substance.

Siphoned into a valve mouth, they were drawn out into a great volcanic courtyard. Starke went close after. He stared down into a black ravine, at the bottom of which was a blazing caldera.

This was the Source Life of the Red Sea. Here it had begun a millennium ago. Here the savage cyclones of sparks and fire energy belched up, shaking titanic black garden walls, causing currents and whirlpools that threatened to suck you forward and shoot you violently up to the surface, in cannulas of force, thrust, in capillaries of ignited mist, in chutes of color that threatened to cremate but only exhilarated you, gave you a seething rebirth!

He braced his legs and fought the suction. An unbelievable sinew of fire sprang up from out the ravine, crackling and roaring.

61

The men of Falga did not fight the attraction.

They moved forward in their silence and hung over the incandescence.

The vitality of the Source grew upward in them. It seemed to touch their sandaled toes first, and then by a process of shining osmosis, climb up the limbs, into the loins, into the vitals, delineating their strong bone structure as mercury delineates the glass thermometer with a rise of temperature. The bones flickered like carved polished ivory through the momentarily film-like flesh. The ribs of a thousand men expanded like silvered spider legs, clenched, then expanded again. Their spines straightened, their shoulders flattened back. Their eyes, the last to take the fire, now were ignited and glowed like candles in refurbished sepulchers. The chins snapped up, the entire outer skins of their bodies broke into silver brilliance.

Swimming through the storm of energy like nightmare figments, entering cold, they reached the far side of the ravine resembling smelted metal from blast furnaces. When they brushed into one another, purple sparks sizzled, jumped from head to head, from hand to hand.

Linnl touched Starke's arm. "You're next."

"No thank you."

"Afraid?" laughed the harp-shepherd. "You're tired. It will give you new life. You're next."

*

Starke hesitated only a moment. Then he let the tide drift him rapidly out. He was afraid. Damned afraid. A belch of fire caught him as he arrived in the core of the ravine. He was wrapped in layers of ecstasy. Beudag pressed against him. It was her consuming hair that netted him and branded him. It was her warmth that crept up his body into his chest and into his head. Somebody yelled somewhere in animal delight and unbearable passion. Somebody danced and threw out his hands and crushed that solar warmth deeper into his huge body. Somebody felt all tiredness, oldness flumed away, a whole new feeling of warmth and strength inserted.

That somebody was Starke.

Waiting on the other side of the ravine were a thousand men of Falga. What sounded like a thousand harps began playing now, and as Starke reached the other side, the harps began marching, and the warriors marched with them. They were still dead, but you would never know it. There were no minds inside those bodies. The bodies were being activated from outside. But you would never know it.

They left the city behind. In embering ranks, the soldier-fighters were led by golden hounds and distant harps to a place where a huge intra-coastal tide swept by.

They got on the tide for a free ride. Linnl beside him, using his harp, Starke felt himself sucked down through a deep where strange monsters sprawled. They looked at Starke with hungry eyes. But the harp wall swept them back.

Starke glanced about at the men. They don't know what they're doing, he thought. Going home to kill their parents and their children, to set the flame to Falga, and they don't know it. Their alive-but-dead faces tilted up, always upward, as though visions of Rann's citadel were there.

Rann. Starke let the wrath simmer in him. He let it cool. Then it was cold. Rann hadn't bothered him now for hours. Was there a chance she'd read his thought in the midst of that fighting nightmare? Did she know this plan for Falga? Was that an explanation for her silence now?

He sent his mind ahead, subtly. *Rann. Rann.* The only answer was the move of silver bodies through the fiery deeps.

63

# LORELEI OF THE RED MIST

Just before dawn they broke the surface of the sea.

Falga drowsed in the red-smeared fog silence. Its slave streets were empty and dew-covered. High up, the first light was bathing Rann's gardens and setting her citadel aglow.

Linnl lay in the shallows beside Starke. They both were smiling half-cruel smiles. They had waited long for this.

Linnl nodded. "This is the day of the carnival. Fruit, wine and love will be offered the returned soldiers of Rann. In the streets there'll be dancing."

Far over to the right lay a rise of mountain. At its blunt peak—Starke stared at it intently—rested a body of a little, scrawny Earthman, with flame-birds clustered on it. He'd climb that mountain later. When it was over and there was time.

"What are you searching for?" asked Linnl.

Starke's voice was distant. "Someone I used to know."

Filing out on the stone quays, their rustling sandals eroded by time, the men stood clean and bright. Starke paced, a caged animal, at their center, so his dark body would pass unnoticed.

They were seen.

The cliff guard looked down over the dirty slave dwellings, from their arrow galleries, and set up a cry. Hands waved, pointed frosty white in the dawn. More guards loped down the ramps and galleries, meeting, joining others and coming on.

Linnl, in the sea by the quay, suggested a theme on the harp. The other harps took it up. The shuddering music lifted from the water and with a gentle firmness, set the dead feet marching down the quays, upward through the narrow, stifling alleys of the slaves, to meet the guard.

Slave people peered out at them tiredly from their choked quarters. The passing of warriors was old to them, of no significance.

# LEIGH BRACKETT AND RAY BRADBURY

These warriors carried no weapons. Starke didn't like that part of it. A length of chain even, he wanted. But this emptiness of the hands. His teeth ached from too long a time of clenching his jaws tight. The muscles of his arms were feverish and nervous.

At the edge of the slave community, at the cliff base, the guard confronted them. Running down off the galleries, swords naked, they ran to intercept what they took to be an enemy.

The guards stopped in blank confusion.

*

A little laugh escaped Starke's lips. It was a dream. With fog over, under and in between its parts. It wasn't real to the guard, who couldn't believe it. It wasn't real to these dead men either, who were walking around. He felt alone. He was the only live one. He didn't like walking with dead men.

The captain of the guard came down warily, his green eyes suspicious. The suspicion faded. His face fell apart. He had lain on his fur pelts for months thinking of his son who had died to defend Falga.

Now his son stood before him. Alive.

The captain forgot he was captain. He forgot everything. His sandals scraped over stones. You could hear the air go out of his lungs and come back in in a numbed prayer.

"My son! In Rann's name. They said you were slain by Faolan's men one hundred darknesses ago. My son!"

A harp tinkled somewhere.

The son stepped forward, smiling.

They embraced. The son said nothing. He couldn't speak.

This was the signal for the others. The whole guard, shocked and surprised, put away their swords and sought out old friends, brothers, fathers, uncles, sons!

They moved up the galleries, the guard and the returned warriors, Starke in their midst. Threading up the cliff, through passage after passage, all talking at once. Or so it seemed. The guards did the talking. None of the dead warriors replied. They only *seemed* to. Starke heard the music strong and clear everywhere.

They reached the green gardens atop the cliff. By this time the entire city was awake. Women came running, bare-breasted and sobbing, and throwing themselves forward into the ranks of their lovers. Flowers showered over them.

"So this is war," muttered Starke, uneasily.

They stopped in the center of the great gardens. The crowd milled happily, not yet aware of the strange silence from their men. They were too happy to notice.

"Now," cried Starke to himself. "Now's the time. Now!"

As if in answer, a wild skirling of harps out of the sky.

The crowd stopped laughing only when the returned warriors of Falga swept forward, their hands lifted and groping before them....

The crying in the streets was like a far siren wailing. Metal made a harsh clangor that was sheathed in silence at the same moment metal found flesh to lie in. A vicious pantomime was concluded in the green moist gardens.

Starke watched from Rann's empty citadel. Fog plumes strolled by the archways and a thick rain fell. It came like a blood squall and washed the garden below until you could not tell rain from blood.

The returned warriors had gotten their swords by now. First they killed those nearest them in the celebration. Then they took the weapons from the victims. It was very simple and very unpleasant.

The slaves had joined battle now. Swarming up from the slave town, plucking up fallen daggers and short swords, they circled the gardens, happening upon the arrogant shining warriors of Rann who had so far escaped the quiet, deadly killing of the alive-but-dead men.

Dead father killed startled, alive son. Dead brother garroted unbelieving brother. Carnival indeed in Falga.

An old man waited alone. Starke saw him. The old man had a weapon, but refused to use it. A young warrior of Falga, harped on by Linnl's harp, walked quietly up to the old man. The old man cried out. His mouth formed words. "Son! What *is* this?" He flung down his blade and made to plead with his boy.

The son stabbed him with silent efficiency, and without a glance at the body, walked onward to find another.

Starke turned away, sick and cold.

A thousand such scenes were being finished.

He set fire to the black spider-silk tapestries. They whispered and talked with flame. The stone echoed his feet as he searched room after room. Rann had gone, probably last night. That meant that Crom Dhu was on the verge of falling. Was Faolan dead? Had the people of Crom Dhu, seeing Beudag's suffering, given in? Falga's harbor was completely devoid of ships, except for small fishing skiffs.

The fog waited him when he returned to the garden. Rain found his face.

The citadel of Rann was fire-encrusted and smoke shrouded as he looked up at it.

A silence lay in the garden. The fight was over.

The men of Falga, still shining with Source-Life, hung their blades from uncomprehending fingers, the light beginning to leave their green eyes. Their skin looked dirty and dull.

Starke wasted no time getting down the galleries, through the slave quarter, and to the quays again.

Linnl awaited him, gently petting the obedient harp.

"It's over. The slaves will own what's left. They'll be our allies, since we've freed them."

Starke didn't hear. He was squinting off over the Red Sea.

Linnl understood. He plucked two tones from the harp, which pronounced the two words uppermost in Starke's thought.

"Crom Dhu."

"If we're not too late." Starke leaned forward. "If Faolan lives. If Beudag still stands at the masthead."

Like a blind man he walked straight ahead, until he fell into the sea.

*

It was not quite a million miles to Crom Dhu. It only seemed that far.

A sweep of tide picked them up just off shore from Falga and siphoned them rapidly, through deeps along coastal latitudes, through crystal forests. He cursed every mile of the way.

He cursed the time it took to pause at the Titan's city to gather fresh men. To gather Clev and Mannt and Aesur and Bruce. Impatiently, Starke watched the whole drama of the Source-Fire and the bodies again. This time it was the bodies of Crom Dhu men, hung like beasts on slow-turned spits, their limbs and vitals soaking through and through, their skins taking bronze color, their eyes holding flint-sparks. And then the harps wove a garment around each, and the garment moved the men instead of the men the garment.

In the tidal basilic now, Starke twisted. Coursing behind him were the new bodies of Clev and Aesur! The current elevated them, poked them through obsidian needle-eyes like spider-silk threads.

There was good irony in this. Crom Dhu's men, fallen at Falga under Conan's treachery, returned now under Conan, to exonerate that treachery.

Suddenly they were in Crom Dhu's outer basin. Shadows swept over them. The long dark falling shadows of Falga's longboats lying in that harbor. Shadows like black culling-nets let down. The school of men cleaved the shadow nets. The tide ceased here, eddied and distilled them.

Starke glared up at the immense silver bottom of a Falgian ship. He felt his face stiffen and his throat tighten. Then, flexing knees, he rammed upward, night air broke dark red around his head.

The harbor held flare torches on the rims of long ships. On the neck of land that led from Crom Dhu to the mainland the continuing battle sounded. Faint cries and clashing made their way through the fog veils. They sounded like echoes of past dreams.

Linnl let Starke have the leash. Starke felt something pressed into his fist. A coil of slender green woven reeds, a rope with hooked weights on the end of it. He knew how to use it without asking. But he wished for a knife, now, even though he realized carrying a knife in the sea was all but impossible if you wanted to move fast.

He saw the sleek naked figurehead of Rann's best ship a hundred yards away, a floating silhouette, its torches hanging fire like Beudag's hair.

He swam toward it, breathing quietly. When at last the silvered figurehead with the mocking green eyes and the flag of shoal-shallow hair hung over him, he felt the cool white ship metal kiss his fingers.

The smell of torch-smoke lingered. A rise of faint shouts from the land told of another rush upon the Gate. Behind him—a ripple. Then—a thousand ripples.

# LORELEI OF THE RED MIST

The resurrected men of Crom Dhu rose in dents and stirrings of sparkling wine. They stared at Crom Dhu and maybe they knew what it was and maybe they didn't. For one moment, Starke felt apprehension. Suppose Linnl was playing a game. Suppose, once these men had won the battle, they went on into Crom Dhu, to rupture Romna's harp and make Faolan the blinder? He shook the thought away. That would have to be handled in time. On either side of him Clev and Mannt appeared. They looked at Crom Dhu, their lips shut. Maybe they saw Faolan's eyrie and heard a harp that was more than these harps that sang them to blade and plunder—Romna's instrument telling bard-tales of the rovers and the coastal wars and the old, living days. Their eyes looked and looked at Crom Dhu, but saw nothing.

The sea shepherds appeared now; the followers of Linnl, each with his harp and the harp music began, high. So high you couldn't hear it. It wove a tension on the air.

Silently, with a grim certainty, the dead-but-not-dead gathered in a bronze circle about Rann's ship. The very silence of their encirclement made your skin crawl and sweat break cold on your cheeks.

A dozen ropes went raveling, looping over the ship side. They caught, held, grapnelled, hooked.

Starke had thrown his, felt it bite and hold. Now he scrambled swiftly, cursing, up its length, kicking and slipping at the silver hull.

He reached the top.

Beudag was there.

Half over the low rail he hesitated, just looking at her.

*

Torchlight limned her, shadowed her. She was still erect; her head was tired and her eyes were closed, her face thinned and less brown,

70

but she was still alive. She was coming out of a deep stupor now, at the whistle of ropes and the grate of metal hooks on the deck.

She saw Starke and her lips parted. She did not look away from him. His breath came out of him, choking.

It almost cost him his life, his standing there, looking at her.

A guard, with flesh like new snow, shafted his bow from the turret and let it loose. A chain lay on deck. Thankfully, Starke took it.

Clev came over the rail beside Starke. His chest took the arrow. The shaft burst half through and stopped, held. Clev kept going after the man who had shot it. He caught up with him.

Beudag cried out. "Behind you, Conan!"

Conan! In her excitement, she gave the old name.

Conan he *was*. Whirling, he confronted a wiry little fellow, chained him brutally across the face, seized the man's falling sword, used it on him. Then he walked in, got the man's jaw, unbalanced him over into the sea.

The ship was awake now. Most of the men had been down below, resting from the battles. Now they came pouring up, in a silver spate. Their yelling was in strange contrast to the calm silence of Crom Dhu's men. Starke found himself busy.

Conan had been a healthy animal, with great recuperative powers. Now his muscles responded to every trick asked of them. Starke leaped cleanly across the deck, watching for Rann, but she was no where to be seen. He engaged two blades, dispatched one of them. More ropes raveled high and snaked him. Every ship in the harbor was exploding with violence. More men swarmed over the rail behind Starke, silently.

Above the shouting, Beudag's voice came, at sight of the fighting men. "Clev! Mannt! Aesur!"

# LORELEI OF THE RED MIST

Starke was a god, anything he wanted he could have. A man's head? He could have it. It meant acting the guillotine with knife and wrist and lunged body. Like—*this*! His eyes were smoking amber and there were deep lines of grim pleasure tugging at his lips. An enemy cannot fight without hands. One man, facing Starke, suddenly displayed violent stumps before his face, not believing them.

Are you watching, Faolan, cried Starke inside himself, delivering blows. Look here, Faolan! God, no, you're blind. *Listen* then! Hear the ring of steel on steel. Does the smell of hot blood and hot bodies reach you? Oh, if you could see this tonight, Faolan. Falga would be forgotten. This is Conan, out of idiocy, with a guy named Starke wearing him and telling him where to go!

It was not safe on deck. Starke hadn't particularly noticed before, but the warriors of Crom Dhu didn't care whom they attacked now. They were beginning to do surgery to one another. They excised one another's shoulders, severed limbs in blind instantaneous obedience. This was no place for Beudag and himself.

He cut her free of the masthead, drew her quickly to the rail.

Beudag was laughing. She could do nothing but laugh. Her eyes were shocked. She saw dead men alive again, lashing out with weapons; she had been starved and made to stand night and day, and now she could only laugh.

Starke shook her.

She did not stop laughing.

"Beudag! You're all right. You're free."

She stared at nothing. "I'll—I'll be all right in a minute."

He had to ward off a blow from one of his own men. He parried the thrust, then got in and pushed the man off the deck, over into the sea. That was the only thing to do. You couldn't kill them.

Beudag stared down at the tumbling body.

72

"Where's Rann?" Starke's yellow eyes narrowed, searching.

"She *was* here." Beudag trembled.

Rann looked out of her eyes. Out of the tired numbness of Beudag, an echo of Rann. Rann was nearby, and this was her doing.

Instinctively, Starke raised his eyes.

Rann appeared at the masthead, like a flurry of snow. Her green-tipped breasts were rising and falling with emotion. Pure hatred lay in her eyes. Starke licked his lips and readied his sword.

Rann snapped a glance at Beudag. Stooping, as in a dream, Beudag picked up a dagger and held it to her own breast.

Starke froze.

Rann nodded, with satisfaction. "Well, Starke? How will it be? Will you come at me and have Beudag die? Or will you let me go free?"

Starke's palms felt sweaty and greasy. "There's no place for you to go. Falga's taken. I can't guarantee your freedom. If you want to go over the side, into the sea, that's your chance. You might make shore and your own men."

"Swimming? With the sea-*beasts* waiting?" She accented the *beasts* heavily. She was one of the sea-*people*. They, Linnl and his men, were sea-*beasts*. "No, Hugh Starke. I'll take a skiff. Put Beudag at the rail where I can watch her all the way. Guarantee my passage to shore and my own men there, and Beudag lives."

Starke waved his sword. "Get going."

He didn't want to let her go. He had other plans, good plans for her. He shouted the deal down at Linnl. Linnl nodded back, with much reluctance.

Rann, in a small silver skiff, headed toward land. She handled the boat and looked back at Beudag all the while. She passed through the sea-beasts and touched the shore. She lifted her hand and brought it smashing down.

# LORELEI OF THE RED MIST

Whirling, Starke swung his fist against Beudag's jaw. Her hand was already striking the blade into her breast. Her head flopped back. His fist carried through. She fell. The blade clattered. He kicked it overboard. Then he lifted Beudag. She was warm and good to hold. The blade had only pricked her breast. A small rivulet of blood ran.

On the shore, Rann vanished upward on the rocks, hurrying to find her men.

In the harbor the harp music paused. The ships were taken. Their crews lay filling the decks. Crom Dhu's men stopped fighting as quickly as they'd started. Some of the bright shining had dulled from the bronze of their arms and bare torsos. The ships began to sink.

Linnl swam below, looking up at Starke. Starke looked back at him and nodded at the beach. "Swell. Now, let's go get that she-devil," he said.

*

Faolan waited on his great stone balcony, overlooking Crom Dhu. Behind him the fires blazed high and their eating sound of flame on wood filled the pillared gloom with sound and furious light.

Faolan leaned against the rim, his chest swathed in bandage and healing ointment, his blind eyes flickering, looking down again and again with a fixed intensity, his head tilted to listen.

Romna stood beside him, filled and refilled the cup that Faolan emptied into his thirsty mouth, and told him what happened. Told of the men pouring out of the sea, and Rann appearing on the rocky shore. Sometimes Faolan leaned to one side, weakly, toward Romna's words. Sometimes he twisted to hear the thing itself, the thing that happened down beyond the Gate of besieged Falga.

Romna's harp lay untouched. He didn't play it. He didn't need to. From below, a great echoing of harps, more liquid than his, like a waterfall drenched the city, making the fog sob down red tears.

74

"Are those harps?" cried Faolan.

"Yes, harps!"

"What was that?" Faolan listened, breathing harshly, clutching for support.

"A skirmish," said Romna.

"Who won?"

"*We* won."

"And *that?*" Faolan's blind eyes tried to see until they watered.

"The enemy falling back from the Gate!"

"And that sound, and that sound!" Faolan went on and on, feverishly, turning this way and that, the lines of his face agonized and attentive to each eddy and current and change of tide. The rhythm of swords through fog and body was a complicated music whose themes he must recognize. "Another fell! I heard him cry. And another of Rann's men!"

"Yes," said Romna.

"But why do our warriors fight so quietly? I've heard nothing from their lips. So quiet."

Romna scowled. "Quiet. Yes—quiet."

"And where did they come from? All our men are in the city?"

"Aye." Romna shifted. He hesitated, squinting. He rubbed his bulldog jaw. "Except those that died at—Falga."

Faolan stood there a moment. Then he rapped his empty cup.

"More wine, bard. More wine."

He turned to the battle again.

"Oh, gods, if I could see it, if I could only see it!"

Below, a ringing crash. A silence. A shouting, a pouring of noise.

"The Gate!" Faolan was stricken with fear. "We've lost! My sword!"

"Stay, Faolan!" Romna laughed. Then he sighed. It was a sigh that did not believe. "In the name of ten thousand mighty gods. Would that I were blind now, or could see better."

Faolan's hand caught, held him. "What *is* it? Tell!"

"Clev! And Tlan! And Conan! And Blucc! And Mannt! Standing in the gate, like wine visions! Swords in their hands!"

Faolan's hand relaxed, then tightened. "Speak their names again, and speak them slowly. And tell the truth." His skin shivered like that of a nervous animal. "You said—Clev? Mannt? Blucc?"

"And Tlan! And Conan! Back from Falga. They've opened the Gate and the battle's won. It's over, Faolan. Crom Dhu will sleep tonight."

Faolan let him go. A sob broke from his lips. "I will get drunk. Drunker than ever in my life. Gloriously drunk. Gods, but if I could have seen it. Been in it. Tell me again of it, Romna...."

*

Faolan sat in the great hall, on his carved high-seat, waiting.

The pad of sandals on stone, outside, the jangle of chains.

A door flung wide, red fog sluiced in, and in the sluice, people walking. Faolan started up. "Clev? Mannt? Aesur!"

Starke came forward into the firelight. He pressed his right hand to the open mouth of the wound on his thigh. "No, Faolan. Myself and two others."

"Beudag?"

"Yes." And Beudag came wearily to him.

Faolan stared. "Who's the other? It walks light. It's a woman."

Starke nodded. "Rann."

Faolan rose carefully from his seat. He thought the name over. He took a short sword from a place beside the high seat. He stepped down. He walked toward Starke. "You brought Rann alive to me?"

Starke pulled the chain that bound Rann. She ran forward in little steps, her white face down, her eyes slitted with animal fury.

"Faolan's blind," said Starke. "I let you live for one damned good reason, Rann. Okay, go ahead."

Faolan stopped walking, curious. He waited.

Rann did nothing.

Starke took her hand and wrenched it behind her back. "I said 'go ahead.' Maybe you didn't hear me."

"I will," she gasped, in pain.

Starke released her. "Tell me what happens, Faolan."

Rann gazed steadily at Faolan's tall figure there in the light.

Faolan suddenly threw his hands to his eyes and choked.

Beudag cried out, seized his arm.

"I can see!" Faolan staggered, as if jolted. "I can see!" First he shouted it, then he whispered it. "*I can see.*"

Starke's eyes blurred. He whispered to Rann, tightly. "Make him see it, Rann or you die now. Make him see it!" to Faolan. "What do you see?"

Faolan was bewildered, he swayed. He put out his hands to shape the vision. "I—I see Crom Dhu. It's a good sight. I see the ships of Rann. Sinking!" He laughed a broken laugh. "I—see the fight beyond the gate!"

Silence swam in the room, over their heads.

Faolan's voice went alone, and hypnotized, into that silence.

He put out his big fists, shook them, opened them. "I see Mannt, and Aesur and Clev! Fighting as they always fought. I see Conan as he was. I see Beudag wielding steel again, on the shore! I see the enemy killed! I see men pouring out of the sea with brown skins and dark hair. Men I knew a long darkness ago. Men that roved the sea with me. *I see Rann captured!*" He began to sob with it, his lungs filling and releasing it, sucking in on it, blowing it out. Tears ran down from his vacant, blazing eyes. "I see Crom Dhu as it was and is and shall be! *I see, I see, I see!*"

Starke felt the chill on the back of his neck.

"I see Rann captured and held, and her men dead around her on the land before the Gate. I see the Gate thrown open—" Faolan halted. He looked at Starke. "Where are Clev and Mannt? Where is Blucc and Aesur?"

Starke let the fires burn on the hearths a long moment. Then he replied.

"They went back into the sea, Faolan."

Faolan's fingers fell emptily. "Yes," he said, heavily. "They had to go back, didn't they? They couldn't stay, could they? Not even for one night of food on the table, and wine in the mouth, and women in the deep warm furs before the hearth. Not even for one toast." He turned. "A drink, Romna. A drink for everyone."

Romna gave him a full cup. He dropped it, fell down to his knees, clawed at his breasts. "My heart!"

"Rann, you sea-devil!"

Starke held her instantly by the throat. He put pressure on the small raging pulses on either side of her snow-white neck. "Let him go, Rann!" More pressure. "*Let him go!*" Faolan grunted. Starke held her until her white face was dirty and strange with death.

It seemed like an hour later when he released her. She fell softly and did not move. She wouldn't move again.

Starke turned slowly to look at Faolan.

"You saw, didn't you, Faolan?" he said.

Faolan nodded blindly, weakly. He roused himself from the floor, groping. "I saw. For a moment, I saw everything. And Gods! but it made good seeing! Here, Hugh-Starke-Called-Conan, give this other side of me something to lean on."

\*

Beudag and Starke climbed the mountain above Falga the next day. Starke went ahead a little way, and with his coming the flame birds scattered, glittering away.

He dug the shallow grave and did what had to be done with the body he found there, and then when the grave was covered with thick grey stones he went back for Beudag. They stood together over it. He had never expected to stand over a part of himself, but here he was, and Beudag's hand gripped his.

He looked suddenly a million years old standing there. He thought of Earth and the Belt and Jupiter, of the joy streets in the Jekkara Low Canals of Mars. He thought of space and the ships going through it, and himself inside them. He thought of the million credits he had taken in that last job. He laughed ironically.

"Tomorrow, I'll have the sea creatures hunt for a little metal box full of credits." He nodded solemnly at the grave. "He wanted that. Or at least he thought. He killed himself getting it. So if the sea people find it, I'll send it up here to the mountain and bury it down under the rocks in his fingers. I guess that's the best place."

Beudag drew him away. They walked down the mountain toward Falga's harbor where a ship waited them. Walking, Starke lifted his face. Beudag was with him, and the sails of the ship were rising to take the wind, and the Red Sea waited for them to travel it. What lay on its far side was something for Beudag and Faolan-of-the-Ships and Romna and Hugh-Starke-Called-Conan to discover. He felt damned good about it. He walked on steadily, holding Beudag near.

# LORELEI OF THE RED MIST

And on the mountain, as the ship sailed, the flame birds soared down fitfully and frustratedly to beat at the stone mound; ceased, and mourning shrilly, flew away.

www.ingramcontent.com/pod-product-compliance
Lightning Source LLC
Chambersburg PA
CBHW031859170626
46807CB00004B/1808